Stalking Yosemite

Abridged Edition

Books by Anne Katherine

Radical Justice
Muir
Stalking Yosemite
<u>Soul Travel Series</u>
The Yesterday Doctor
Explosions
The Rock Chief

Nonfiction

Boundaries: Where You End and I Begin
Where to Draw the Line
When Misery is Company
The Splintered Cross
Boundaries in an Overconnected World
Anatomy of a Food Addiction
How to Make Almost Any Diet Work
Your Appetite Switch
Lick It! Fix Her Appetite Switch
4 Changes: Fix Your Eating and Fix Your Life

Stalking Yosemite

Abridged Edition

John Muir Battles the Second Assault on Yosemite

America Not For Sale

Anne Katherine

STALKING YOSEMITE - Abridged Edition
This is a work of historical and biographical fiction based primarily on the books of John Muir, which are in the public domain.

Additional sources include Yosemite legend, the Sierra Club website, classes at the Gilder Lehrman Institute of American History, the National Park Service, California Digital Library, and the author's imagination.   A complete Bibliography is in the Appendix.

Cover Photo Credit: Anne Katherine
Back Cover Photo Credit: Sherry Ascher
Rufous Hummingbird Photo: Used by Permission by Albert Rose, https://www.albertrose.com
Italicized Chapter Subtitles are quotes from John Muir and cited in the Endnotes.

ISBN: 979-8-9903227-2-1
9 8 7 6 5 4 3 2

To Jim Webster

His passing leaves an ache in the heart. A good, good man has flown his last flight from this grieving earth.

1941-2021

Dedication

To National Park Service Staff
Both Volunteer and Paid

For your passion, dedication, and sacrifice.

The Second Assault on Yosemite

Is America For Sale?

Yosemite is one of the most exquisite of Earth's natural gifts. If she isn't safe, nothing is.

The first assault on Yosemite occurred in 1851, when the Mariposa Battalion invaded the Valley in order to either corral or kill the native people.

The second organized, ruthless assault on Yosemite National Park flared in 1903, although the wheels started turning more than a decade before.

In each case, the motive was greed, dressed in more beguiling garments.

This is that story.

Table of Contents

Italicized Chapter Titles are all from John's own words.

Maps of Yosemite

Yosemite Boundaries 1890 and 1905[1]

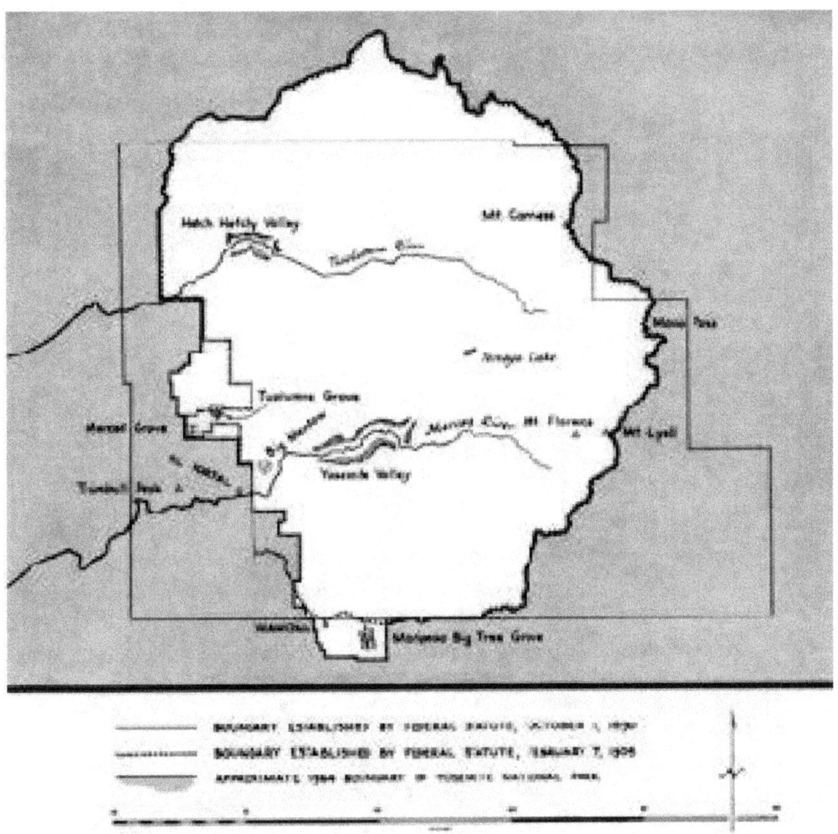

Rectangular box: 1890 boundary when Yosemite became a National Park.

White territory: the area protected by the 1905 boundary. This organic revision was designed and promoted by John Muir.

Hetch Hetchy Valley, left, on upper third, and **Yosemite Valley,** just left of center, on the bottom third, are defined with parallel lines around their respective rivers.

USGS Survey Map of Yosemite, 1900[2]

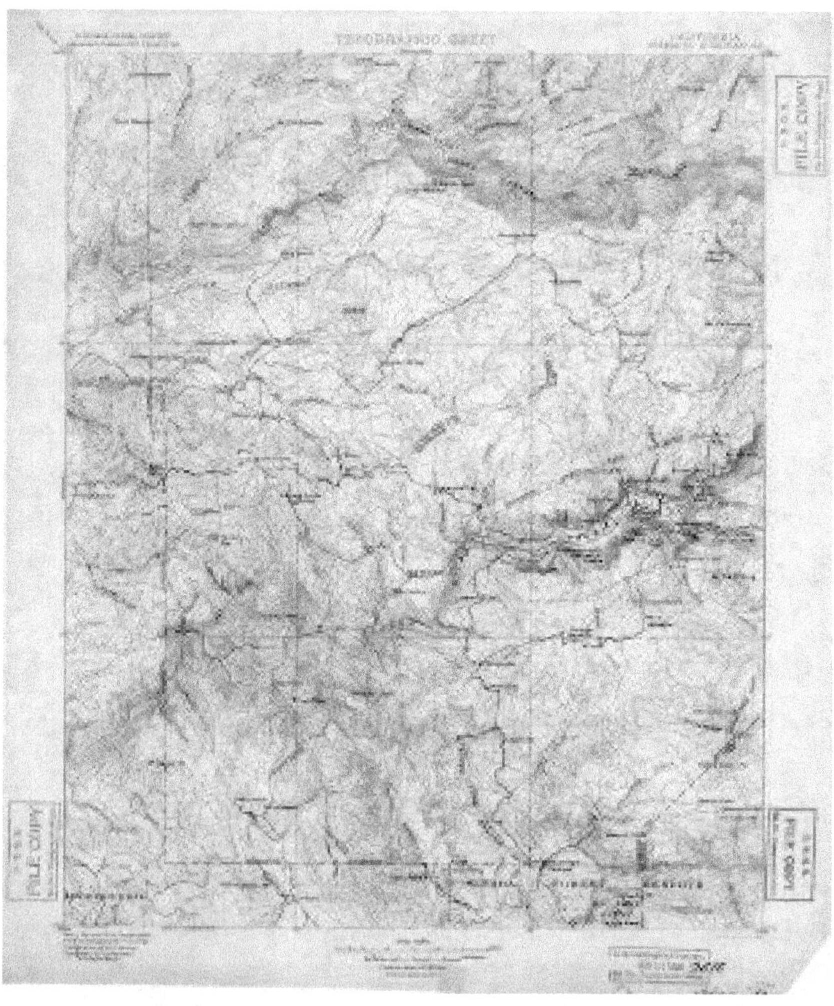

Yosemite Valley is the area of darker parallel lines, right of center, near the middle of the page.

Hetch Hetchy Valley is the darker area near the top of the page.

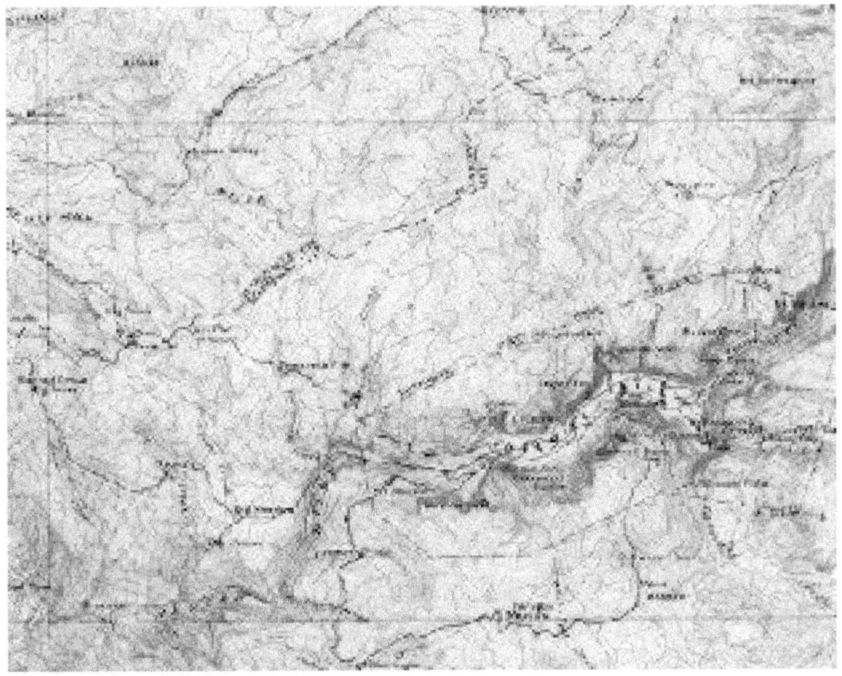

A closeup of the USGS map shows the boundary lines of Yosemite Valley as a California State Park in 1900.

Muir/Roosevelt Locations and Camping Spots[3]

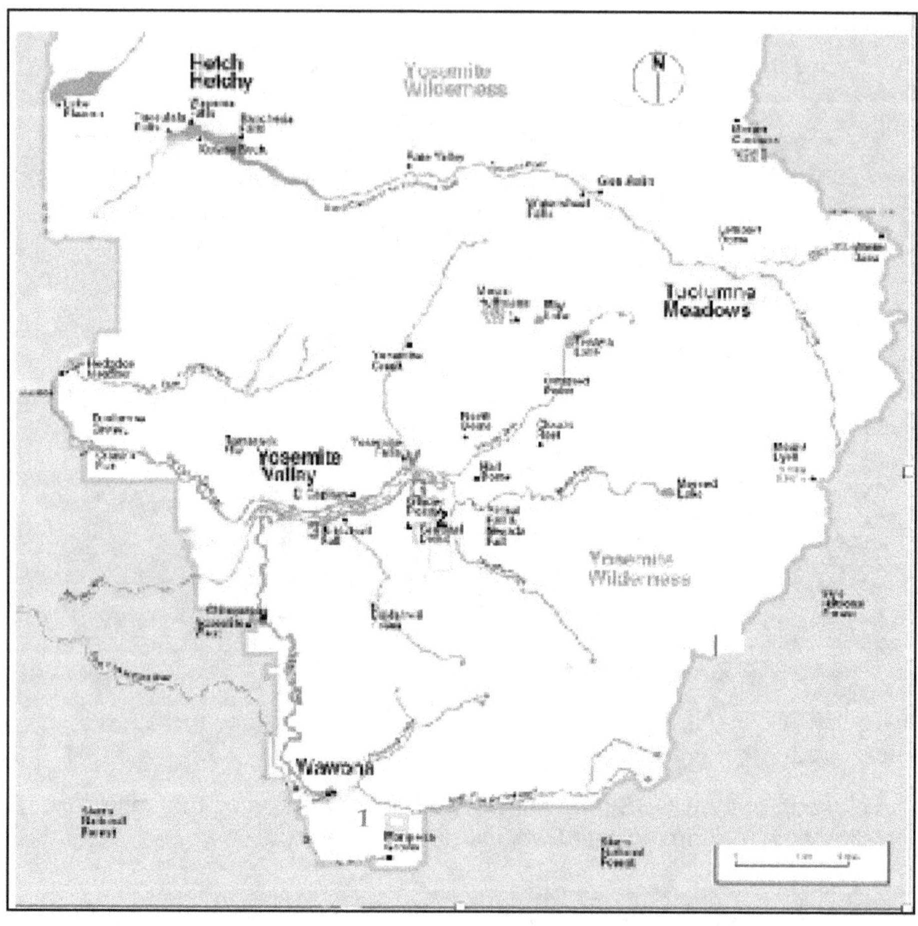

W -- Day 1. Wawona
1 -- Night 1, in Mariposa Grove (elevation c6000')
G -- Day 2, Glacier Point (7000')
2 -- Night 2, at Sentinel Dome. (Those present disagree on
precise location, but in general between Sentinel Dome and
Glacier Point. Number is placed at a relatively flat area.)
V -- Day 3, Yosemite Valley (4000')
3 -- Night 3, below Bridalveil fall (3900')

Rufous Hummingbird
Albert Rose[4]

"I have never yet happened on a trace of evidence...that any one animal was ever made for another as much as it was made for itself."

John Muir[5]

1
Situation Normal
USA
1850-1903

MESA VERDE

Near a cliff dwelling, two unappealing scavengers in a roughly oval hole, throw their shovels up to the ground and lift a skeleton onto a canvas tarp alongside the pit.

At a roadside *Museum*, the skeleton, wired, propped upright, holds a sign: 'Cold Drinks.'

THE GRAND CANYON

A Guide, standing on the rim, aims his rifle at a soaring eagle. Behind him, 10 tourists aim firearms at the eagle.

Multiple gunshots echo throughout the canyon.

The dead bird plummets to the canyon floor.

ROCKY MOUNTAINS

Billboards obscure much of the scenery: "Game Park: Shoot your First Elk." "Hunting Lodge - You Kill It, We'll Cook It." "Homestead Plots For Sale." "Game Reserve." "Guided Hunting."

SMOKY MOUNTAINS

Loggers strip trees from a mountainside.

2
Hetch Hetchy
1890s

Waterfalls splashed into a beautiful, dramatic glacier-carved Valley with a clear meandering river.

Alongside the river, a small village of o'chums (conical bark huts) circled a lovely meadow.

Wil-Tuk-Umee families surrounded a dying fire. Within the fire were bone fragments in the shape of a skeleton.

The women had long, shiny black hair and wore skirts of dressed deer-skin, fringed, from the waist to their knees.

The men wore a hip skirt made of skins. All wore plain moccasins on their feet. Young children were nude. All were clean.

Wa-Le-Co, in his 20s, gold skin, black hair and eyes, stood solemnly. Tears saturated his cheeks.

Ha-Ky-Me, his wife, pregnant, held him with her arm around his waist. Toddler An-Si, 3 years old, their son, hugged Wa-Le-Co's legs.

The fire burned down to ash, no longer smoking. Men reverently placed the charred bones into a dug hole.

The Grandmother, face wet with tears, leaned over

the pit and cut her hair into it, then took ashes from the
fire, mixed them with pine pitch and smeared them on
her face. Food, clothing, a bow, and blanket were all
added for the use of the Grandfather's spirit.

Wa-Le-Co started to run up a steep trail next to the
Tuolumne River. Man-Nik, his uncle, in his 40s,
approached. Man-Nik opened his arms.

Wa-Le-Co slammed into his uncle's chest and
sobbed. Then he pulled himself back and ran up the
narrow trail to the east.

At the high elevation, Wa-Le-Co loped across an
exquisite meadow. He heard a man laughing joyously.

Wa-Le-Co immediately concealed himself.

A poorly dressed white scarecrow, John Muir, in his
50s, with unruly gray-streaked auburn hair and beard,
grinned at pikas, who'd laid lupines to dry on a boulder.
They gathered their little bundles and took them into
their underground passages.

Muir rose and sauntered across the meadow. Wa-Le-
Co followed silently, watchful and suspicious.

Clouds gathered overhead.

On a wagon trail forested on both sides, Big Oak Flat
Road, horses walked in cadence, leather creaking,
brasses clinking.

Muir jumped down to the road to greet Col. Samuel
Baldwin M. Young, a white man in his 50s, bushy
mustache, hat at a jaunty angle, at the head of a line of

US Cavalry.

Young and Muir shook hands, regarded each other with respect.

Wa-Le-Co watched, hidden, his face dark and angry.

The last time a battalion entered the Valley, they were intent on capturing or killing the people born here. They killed the youngest son of the great chief, Tenaya, only 30 summers ago.

Wa-Le-Co watched as the Army continued down the Sierra toward the Yosemite Valley, and as the other white man headed in the direction of one of the Sequoia groves, then he whirled and ran hard, back to his Hetch Hetchy Valley.

3
No Race Prejudice
Market Street
San Francisco - Summer - 1890

Former Governor George Perkins paraded down a wide sidewalk made of long cross-wise boards. At his side marched James Phelan,[6] banker, in his 30s, dedicated to the growth of San Francisco.

Market Street was moderately busy with horse-drawn vehicles.

The two white men approached a knot of Chinese men wearing dragon caps, standing close to the curb.

Phelan slammed into the Chinese men, causing some to fall into the street. Horses neighed. A wagon cart clipped a carriage.

The two distinguished men continued without looking back, missing that Chinese men waved angry arms and yelled, "Ben dan!" and "Báigui," which mean stupid and white demon.

Perkins said, "Those aliens, a curse to this country, Mr. Phelan. Of course, I don't have race prejudice."

"Neither do I, Governor Perkins."

Perkins noted, "Same problem as with the Hopi."

"The Indians? How so?

"Even when we sent them to Alcatraz, they refused to

farm the way the Federal government commanded, and they resisted surrendering their children to government boarding schools."

The two men turned to a side street and walked up a steep hill.

Phelan understood. "We have to weaken their clan and tribal structures."

4
Bad News

Elegant Men's Club
San Francisco - Fall - 1890

Phelan, his face an angry red, entered the private room carrying a rolled newspaper like a club. He tromped to the bar, and slapped the marble with his palm.

The white bartender grabbed an expensive Scotch and slopped it into a shot glass. Phelan knocked it down and held the glass out for another.

Phelan thwacked the paper club onto the small table where sat Governor Perkins and the pompous Esquire Donald Campbell. "Have you seen this, Perkins?"

Phelan unfurled the paper and pointed to the headline: "51ST CONGRESS DECREE 26. STATUTE 650, CHAPTER 1263, OCTOBER 1, 1890"

Perkins nodded, "Sadly, Mr. Phelan, I have. Congress has established three National Parks: Sequoia, General Grant...and Yosemite."

Phelan was outraged, "To claim any more land within 42 townships is now impossible for all time!"

Campbell growled, "And John Muir is responsible."

John Howard, officer of a large investment firm, strode in.

Phelan turned toward him. "Did you hear, Howard?

Jo—"

Howard grabbed a jar of boiled eggs and lobbed it into a wall. Glass, eggshells, cooked yellow and white fragments rebounded into the room and onto the carpet.

Perkins said, drily, "I do believe he has heard."

Howard barked, "Timber, grazing pastures, and mines."

Liveried men scurried to clean up Howard's mess. Howard showed no concern about them. He sat, furious.

Phelan said, "Paper, lumber, wool, and minerals. Obviously you had investments there."

Campbell said, "Muir snuck up on us."

Howard growled, "Now we sneak up on him."

5
Reconnaissance
Yosemite
Big Oak Flat Road

Donald Campbell and John Howard, plus six white men on horseback—boots too shiny, wool coats too clean—trotted their horses along Big Oak Flat Road.

They all had rifles sticking from their scabbards, pistols in their holsters.

The eight riders slowed their steeds, wary, looking ahead. They watched Elwell, their hunting guide, a rough mountain man with a long scruffy beard, on mule back. Elwell held his hand up to signal: Halt!

The riders, all watchful, brought their horses to a stop.

Elwell yanked his rifle from its scabbard and handed it over to John Howard. He then turned his mule broadside to the other riders and sliced his lips with his flat perpendicular hand. With his other perpendicular hand, he motioned sideways, as if to push the men off the trail. The mounted men turned their steeds silently to the left, and sneaked into the woods.

Elwell then rode alone, around several curves, to a guard booth.

Sergeant George Goodrich stepped to the door.

"Remember, Elwell, no firearms allowed. No hunting or harvesting in a National Park."

Elwell patted the empty scabbard, slapped palms on his sides to show the absence of a holster or pistol. "On my own, George. My clients have abandoned their plans."

Goodrich nodded. Elwell trotted his mule on into the Park. Goodrich watched him, eyes narrowed.

At Hetch Hetchy, Campbell, Howard, and the other six men spread out. One man took a pickax to a canyon wall. Another twisted a limb roughly, splintering it, off a perfectly symmetrical incense cedar. A third used a string to measure the circumference of a Ponderosa Pine, then loudly calculated the board feet it would yield. Some kneeled beside the Tuolumne River and tasted the water.

The men saw all in their view as a commodity, beauty of little account.

That night, sparks lifted up to the stars that put black mountain silhouettes in relief. The eight tidy men and scruffy Elwell relaxed around a large, wasteful, white man's campfire, the firelight painting their faces.

A spit over the fire held a roasting animal—illegally shot. Elwell turned the spit. Dripping fat sizzled in the fire.

Donald Campbell turned to a man who had only ever known privilege. "Now that you see Hetch Hetchy first hand, what do you think, Mr.—"

The man gave Campbell a warning look. Campbell back-pedaled, correctly interpreting the man's desire to remain anonymous. "Mr. Utilities."

The other men laughed, understanding the transaction.

Mr. Utilities said, "Next time I'm bringing my cook. No offense Elwell."

Campbell asked, "Isn't he Chinese?"

Mr. Utilities grumbled, "We're not eating *him*, Campbell."

Howard quipped, "Not that Governor Perkins would have a problem with that."

Campbell added, "Nor would Phelan."

The men laughed, entirely comfortable with racism. A bottle of whiskey passed from hand to hand. Mr. Utilities stood and surveyed the narrow valley. "As the engineers said, narrow valley opening, easily dammed. An endless quantity of water. Perfect."

Four dark eyes watched the white men. Wa-Le-Co and Man-nik sat like boulders inside a thick bush. When they glanced at each other, their fear and grief showed.

Mr. Lumber Tycoon asked, "Does John Muir know what you're up to? Right under his nose?"

Campbell answered, "No. And we have his own myopia on our side. He hates cities and large groups, he's happy to leave all the legalese to professionals, and if you gave him a choice between a naked woman, a pile of money, or a weed—"

Howard finished, "He'd pick the weed."

Campbell qualified, "Well, he'd choose it, but first he'd sit and stare at it for two days."

The men laughed.

Man-nik and Wa-Le-Co narrowed eyes. These men were the enemy of their enemy, but that first enemy was a man who had brought an army.

6
Leaving Home
Steep Trail to Tuolumne

The Hetch Hetchy People climbed the dusty trail. They all, even the children, wore baskets holding their tools, weapons, and food. They were moving.

As they rounded a switchback, they paused and looked below. And wept. Even the children, who had started the day excited about an adventure, understood they were abandoning home.

They trudged upward, helping the elders and the Grandmother.

Ha-Ky-Me reached up and grabbed a boulder for leverage as she rounded a narrow switchback close to the edge. The boulder tilted. Ha-Ky-Me dangled and screamed. Wa-Le-Co leapt toward her, but the boulder released.

Men held Wa-Le-Co hard. Man-Nik grabbed An-Si as he ran toward the cliff edge for his mother, whose long diminishing scream ended in a distant thud.

Wa-Le-Co fell to his knees. "Ken! Ha-Ky-Me!"

Because his enemy had brought an Army, and his People had to flee their Place, his wife and unborn child had been killed. His enemy was the First Cause of his wife's death.

7
Cloaking the Motive
Private Men's Club - 1903

Campbell, Mr. Utilities, Perkins—now a U.S. Senator—
and Phelan, previous mayor of San Francisco, sat
comfortably in leather chairs in a spacious circle.

William Randolph Hearst, the wealthy inventor of
Yellow Journalism, fake interviews, and doctored
pictures, strutted in. The men all rose with alacrity, as if
he were a king.

Phelan stepped forward to shake Hearst's hand. "Mr.
Hearst. How's your newspaper business?"

"Expanding coast-to-coast, Mayor Phelan."

They both sat. The white waiter brought Hearst a
whiskey.

Phelan said, "President Roosevelt is coming to San
Francisco."

Howard added, "We want the President on our side."

Mayor Phelan complained, "Interior Secretary
Hitchcock has already turned down our application for a
dam—twice."

Senator Perkins grumbled, "Turned me down too.
1898. I introduced legislation to build a railroad into the
Yosemite Valley."

Mr. Utilities asked, "What were you gonna do with a

railroad?"

"Timber cutting. Possible coal deposits." Perkins spit into his whiskey glass, disgusted.

Hearst said, "That's your problem."

Insulted, Perkins bristled.

Hearst continued, "Don't reveal what you're really after. Make the peasants think they're getting something. Howard, what is your estimate of the value of contracts for developing Hetch Hetchy."

"Over $100 million."

Hearst waved toward the east. "Drum got his railway approved to El Portal, didn't he, Campbell?"

Campbell nodded.

"How'd he present it?"

"Cut travel to Yosemite by an entire day. Travel comfortably by train instead of by bumpy stagecoach."

"Why'd he really want it?"

Mr. Utilities answered, "Timber and that new mine in El Portal."

Hearst asked, "Why do you want Hetch Hetchy?"

The men answered as one, "Power."

Hearst laughed. "Consensus—often sought and rarely found. However, you have a problem. Housewives are scared of electricity. And their husbands, that pay utility bills, don't consider electricity essential."

Campbell asserted, "Electricity *is* dangerous."

Senator Perkins shrugged, "So the world loses some

little people."

Hearst brushed that comment aside. "Each child born creates another hungry mouth to feed and every atom of humanity added to the struggling mass means another figure in our bank accounts."

He waved toward Mr. Utilities. "People don't care about electricity. They do care about water. That's the approach to take."

Mayor Phelan smiled, "I just happen to have bought up the riparian rights to the Tuolumne River."

Hearst saluted Phelan with his shot glass.

8
Alhambra

Martinez, CA - March, 1903

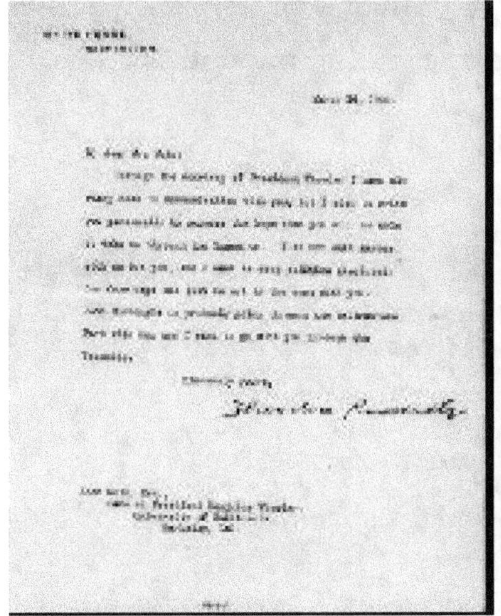

White House, Washington
March 14, 1903.

My dear Mr. Muir:
Through the courtesy of
President Wheeler I have
already been in communication
with you, but I wish to write
you personally to express the
hope that you will be able to
take me through the Yosemite.
I do not want anyone with me
but you....

Sincerely yours,
Theodore Roosevelt

John Muir, 64, neat white beard to his sternum, well dressed in a good wool suit, vest, and heavy watch chain, crackled with energy.

He paced his scribble den,[7] dodging piles of papers

and books. He waved a letter in the air. "I'm driven out of my mind by all these letters, telegrams, phone calls." He pulled on his hair, gestured at his desk, irritated. "All insisting that I guide Theodore Roosevelt through The Yosemite."

Louise Strentzel Muir, 54, his wife and a strong Muir champion, sat next to the fire. Her dark hair was pulled like a curtain to either side of her face. She wore a long dark dress, lace collar. "Have you answered?"

He rifled his desk papers and pulled one out. He read out loud.

> *March 1903*
> *Dear Senator Rowell,*
> *I see that the President's little raid into the Yosemite is to be made after the middle of May.*
> *I shall not be able to join in it. Please convey my regrets to the President.*
> *Faithfully yours,*
> *John Muir*[8]

She winced.

He flung the letter onto the desk.

"Many would consider this an honor, John."

He halted and looked full at her. "You think I should do it!"

"You have two passions. Your strongest and deepest

is your peerless gift—your ability to connect with a single tree or a single bird, to enter that life force as a brother, with love and an awareness hardly any other human has."

He flopped into a chair close to hers.

"Your other passion is the wilderness itself. The entirety of it. I think this is your great opportunity to gain the protection you crave for the Wilderness you love. If you could manage to be as moderate in your words as you are in your articles—well, most of them."

He used both hands to gently pull her hand close so he could kiss it. "I have three passions."

He dashed to his desk and scribbled.

He then stood, his back arched, in an orator's pose. "How's this:"

> *Dear Sargent,*
> *An influential man from*
> *Washington wants to make a trip*
> *into the Sierra with me, and I might*
> *be able to do some forest good in*
> *talking freely around the campfire.*[9]

She laughed. Then she leaned forward, "Remember one thing, John—"

He pivoted and listened closely.

9
Welcome President Theodore Roosevelt

Raymond, California, Train Terminal - May 15, 1903

Red, white, and blue bunting swallowed the station. On the skirting, a band played boisterous patriotic music. Little boys marched straight-armed like miniature soldiers.

President Theodore Roosevelt, 45, robust and manly, waved from the extended platform at the rear of his special train. The train was decorated gaily and had a large picture of Roosevelt.

He paused at the top of the three ladder-like steps. His elevated hand still upright, no longer waving, as he scanned the crowd.

When his gaze passed a section of crowd, that section called and waved, but he was not connecting. He was searching for someone.

An experienced politician, his surprise and disbelief —at not finding the person he sought—were hidden.

Waving again, he descended to the graveled roadbed and crossed to an 11-passenger, open, mule-drawn stage. He climbed onto the front port-side bench, to sit next to his driver, Bright Gillespie, somewhere in his 40's. Gillespie immediately flipped the reins. The stage creaked and rattled uphill. Roosevelt leaned over to shout to Gillespie.

"Is Mr. Muir ever where he supposed to be?"

Gillespie shouted back, "According to his own lights, yes."

Men convinced of their own importance and pretending to ignore the crowd were crammed into the back bench seats. All wore linen dusters.

"Mr. Muir will join us, right?"

Gillespie shrugged his shoulders high. The stage clopped along.

10
Wilderness Meadow

John Muir, his hair and beard unruly, sat in a snowy meadow and communed with a raspberry-like Snow plant.

11
When David Was King
Mariposa Sequoia Grove - May 15, 1903

"I expected him at last night's reception in San Francisco, but he never showed up."

Gillespie, reins in hands, spread his palms—like waddaya gonna do? He clicked the mules into a clearing surrounded by Jeffrey pines, their vanilla scent gentle on the air.

Roosevelt scanned the clearing.

Thirty mounted cavalry under Lieutenant Mays lined the perimeter, horses facing inward. They sat at attention. As the stage lurched to a stop, the Cavalrymen saluted as one.

A second stage creaked to a halt behind Gillespie's, carrying Zach and Elias, Treasury men, both armed, in wool shirts and boots; and LeConte, the photographer, with his photographic equipment.

Ranger Charles Leidig, rugged, friendly, stepped forward to grab the bridle of the lead mule. "Welcome to the Mariposa Grove of Sequoias, Gentlemen." He wore the state ranger uniform: a long double-breasted belted jacket, trousers tucked into boots, and a ranger hat.

John Muir stepped out from between two trees of the

surrounding forest and sauntered toward the stage, leading two saddled mules.

Roosevelt spotted Muir and jumped down. Roosevelt wore a bandanna around his neck, a Norfolk jacket, baggy breeches tucked into leather puttees, and a tall brimmed hat—masculine stylish.

Muir looked like a tramp. He wore a stretched and soiled wool business suit, a wrinkled and bunched vest, and an old felt hat—guilelessly unstylish.

Leidig snorted a laugh.

Gillespie chuckled. "You didn't think John would change his outfit for a mere President of the United States, did you?"

Roosevelt and Muir each took a step toward the other.

Leidig leaned toward Gillespie. "The Hunter and the Naturalist face off."

Muir handed the reins of the darker mule to Roosevelt, who mounted easily and clucked the mule in a wide circle. The President sat the mule as comfortably as a sofa.

Muir studied Roosevelt's conformation.

Leidig whispered to Bright, "Muir is testing a President's form?"

Gillespie whispered back, "A President who was in the cavalry?" He pointed, "Look, the President perceives Muir's appraisal."

Roosevelt studied Muir as Muir studied Roosevelt's riding. Roosevelt's entire demeanor revealed his deep comprehension of Muir's behavior.

Roosevelt got the look of a boy about to have some fun.

Muir and Roosevelt rode side-by-side up the curving wagon road.

As they rounded tree-filled gullies, the two men could hear the clomping hoofbeats and creaking stage following them. Louder even than a scolding raven, those men were out-talking each other, a male pecking-order competition.

Muir turned his mule sideways to block a steep, narrow trail. He nodded toward the sounds from the stage, then to Roosevelt. His eyes twinkled. "We can take the stage road if this trail is too rugged for you, Mr. President Rough Rider."

Roosevelt shot Muir a squelching glance, steered his mule around Muir's and up the trail.

When the trail widened, Muir brought his mule alongside Roosevelt's.

The President said, "You do know I'm a cavalry man."

"Yup."

"You were testing my form."

"Mule is in my charge," said Muir, calmly.

Surprised, Roosevelt swiveled his head to look at Muir, who was peacefully studying a squirrel spiraling up a tree. Muir grinned at him.

The President huffed, "I'm used to a little more

pandering."

Muir hee-hawed. Roosevelt tried to hide a smile.

The trail turned and suddenly dropped them into the Sequoia Grove.

Muir announced, "Mr. President, I introduce you to," he stood in his stirrups for a two-arm flourish, "The Sequoias."

Roosevelt, negotiating the last twist of trail, spoke before looking, "Call me Colonel."

Then he lifted his eyes and went still.

Roosevelt craned his neck to see the treetops. With a hushed voice, he said, "No description does them justice."

"Men clamor and strive," Muir gestured, "But these sentinels, silent and peaceful, breathed the last exhale of Christ. They felt the echoes of the Magna Carta and rode the tsunami of the Declaration of Independence."[10]

John led Roosevelt up to the Grizzly Giant. Roosevelt came to a dead stop.

"Aye, this tree." Muir backed up to sit on a boulder. "This tree was alive during the reign of King David of Israel." Roosevelt shook his head, taking in such longevity.

"D'ya think, p'haps, tiz worth protectin'?" added John.

Too quickly, the stage rattled over the last hump of the road. Dignitaries clambered from the stage and pattered toward Roosevelt, their focus the President.

Muir shook his head. "Your followers ignore giants."

"You imply I'm not a giant." The President seemed miffed.

Muir gave Roosevelt a measuring look, uncertain. Roosevelt glanced at Muir, consisting of *two can play this game*.

Muir stooped to pick up a tiny sequoia cone and fed it through Roosevelt's buttonhole. The President recoiled, displeased. He brushed the cone off his chest.

While LeConte set up a large camera facing the Grizzly Giant, Roosevelt introduced some of the pillars to Muir.

A relaxed man in a Norfolk jacket, like Roosevelt dressed for the woods, approached. Roosevelt smiled spontaneously, "John, meet my good friend, the President of Columbia University, Dr. Nicholas Butler."

Governor Pardee shouldered out Butler, his posture showing his belief in his own greater importance.

Roosevelt and Butler flicked quick eye contact with each other, both way too polished to show judgment.

"Mr. Muir, meet George Pardee, the Governor of California."

Pardee, vacuous expression, the only dignitary still wearing a linen duster, ignored Muir. John sized him up and was visibly unimpressed.

"Welcome, Mr. President, to California's first State Park." Pardee spoke proudly as if he'd planted the sequoias himself. Muir jerked his head at the words *state park*. Roosevelt registered this.

As the various men approached Roosevelt, most in three piece wool suits, Roosevelt immediately became urbane. "Gentlemen! Welcome to the great sequoia grove."

Muir shook his head in disgust, leapt up the trail leading away from the Giant, turned, and squatted to watch as the men toadied for the President's attention.

Zach, a broad thinker, leaned against the side of the Grizzly Giant. Elias watched from the back side of the tree. John Howard tied a horse in the woods and stepped next to Elias.

Howard asked him quietly, "Are you the governor?"

"Secret Service. Me and Zach guard the President." Elias pointed, "There's the governor."

"The pot needs more pepper," said Howard.

Elias looked around, for a pot.

Howard stepped forward. "President Roosevelt, I bear an invitation from a club of important Gentlemen. I believe you are a member. To honor your Big Five title, we would like to host you on a mountain lion hunt." Howard offered his hand.

Roosevelt shook it. "Thank you, Mr.—"

"John Howard."

"Thank you, Mr. Howard, I would like that very much."

Muir's face shifted dramatically to aversion.

Howard faded back into the woods.

Roosevelt called, "John come back down here." He

faced the group and made a courtly gesture. "Gentlemen, I introduce you to John Muir, of the University of Wisconsin and the University of the Wilderness."

Most of the men looked Muir over, at his wrinkled and baggy suit, with degrees of dismissiveness. Butler was amused and impishly showed them their error. "I've read your eloquent articles, Sir. Please sign me up to your Sierra Club."

Muir nodded at Butler's acknowledgment, but turned away without speaking. Roosevelt and Butler exchanged a glance.

The men lined up in front of the Grizzly Giant. Roosevelt backed into the row close to Muir. Muir very quietly edged sideways, closer to Butler's shoulder. Roosevelt glanced knowingly at Muir, then faced forward.

The photographer instructed, "Hold still please, Gentlemen."

Elias, Grizzly Giant, Zach, Secretary of the Navy, Pardee, Roosevelt,
Dr. Rixie, Muir, Butler, Secretary Loeb, U of CA Pres. Wheeler,
Grizzly Giant

When LeConte said the men could relax, Roosevelt
faced the entire group. "Gentlemen, go back to the
hotel. Enjoy the banquet laid out for you."

The Dignitaries headed for their stage. Muir
escaped into an alley between the enormous trees.
Zach and Elias lingered. The Cavalry stayed put.

The President waved toward the Cavalry, Zach, and
Elias. "You also. Thank you for your service. God bless
you."

The Cavalrymen saluted, turned their horses, and left
in formation. Zach and Elias looked at each other,
shrugged, and walked downhill.

Wa-Le-Co sat his Appaloosa in the woods. He watched the cavalry file down the road. He pulled his breech-loading single shot rifle, checked the chamber, snapped it shut, and sighted on Lieutenant Mays.

His rifle barrel followed each Army man as he rode past. He put his finger on the trigger.

Then Wa-Le-Co shook his head and held the rifle across the withers of his horse.

In the grove, Roosevelt looked around to find himself alone. Their mules were tied at the side, so he knew John was still here.

He stepped up toward the tunnel tree, paused, and listened. His instincts as a warrior told him to go up, so he continued through the tunnel tree upward.

He found John sauntering ahead of him.

"What's the Big Five title?" asked Muir.

Roosevelt hesitated, unusual for him. "Lion, African Elephant, Cape Buffalo, African Leopard, Rhinoceros."

Muir said, coldly, "Slaughtered?"

Roosevelt answered immediately, "Yes."

"Ye needed that leopard to feed your family, did ye?"

"Would it help to know the elephant went rogue in a village, killing a child?"

John bent over with one hand clutching his face and the other arm across his stomach. He put his hands on his knees, and bent over more, as if wounded. He panted deeply.

"Had that elephant seen her child or her sister killed by men?"

Roosevelt got thoughtful, a point of view that had not ever struck him.

John loped forward, leaving Roosevelt behind, and stretched his arms across the trunk of a sequoia: an embrace, a hug.

Roosevelt was startled yet again.

Muir stuck his nose into a groove in the bark and inhaled. The sequoia restored Muir. His natural inner joy resurfaced. Muir challenged, "Smell this tree. I dare you to describe its fragrance."

Roosevelt glanced back at their shadows--Ranger Leidig and Ranger Archie Leonard. Roosevelt regarded the tree. "I've hugged my horse. But hug a tree? Doesn't seem quite the manly thing to do."

Muir nodded with a measuring look. He sniffed the tree again, a hearty inhale. Muir studied Roosevelt, "You are careful of your image."

Roosevelt studied Muir. "You are not."

Both comments sounded like insults.

12
The Meaning of Secret
Wawona Big Trees Hotel

The welcoming veranda was decorated with American flags that had 45 stars in their blue fields.

Howard walked up the steps as Mr. Utilities exited the hotel. "Assessment?"

"Muir is indeed unpolished and rude, but the contrast to the boot-lickers intrigues the President."

"The President is amused by the farm boy? Not good." Worried, Mr. Utilities put his fist to his mouth and thought. "Them together three days could be dangerous for us."

"Even though Roosevelt already declared he was on our side?"

Mr. Utilities paced up and down the long veranda. "John Muir is our enemy. Who else could lead Roosevelt through these...assets?"

"A ranger?"

"So Roosevelt could still have his fun if Muir were... removed."

Zach and Elias emerged from the barn, arguing.

Howard chin-pointed, "At least I discovered—those are the Treasury men."

Howard led Mr. Utilities to the far end of the veranda.

The two men went silent as Zach and Elias climbed the steps to the front door.

Elias shouted, "Hey Zach, a fellow thought I was the governor."

Zach, intensely skeptical, said, "Who?"

"Some fella. And then something about peppering a pot. At that huge tree. He was gonna pepper something."

Zach shook his head. "Elias, there's no way anyone seriously thought you were the governor. He was snaking out your function. You told him you were Secret Service, didn't you?"

Elias looked guilty.

"Do you know what secret means, Elias?"

Elias looked guiltier. They entered the hotel.

Mr. Utilities was disbelieving, "The Treasury agents are here? At the hotel?"

"Roosevelt dismissed them."

"Finally, some luck."

13
Understand This Tree?
Galen Clark Cabin

Roosevelt and Muir lounged against the edge of the porch.

Muir spoke as if he were continuing a conversation started moments ago, "I would not want you to think I claim an honor I do not have. I did not actually receive a degree from the University of Wisconsin."

"Dr. Whitney proclaimed that to the great world already. You made an enemy there."

Muir, sublimely unconcerned about his reputation, swept his arm, denoting the stately sequoia trees ringing the cabin. "The Guardians. Sit in quiet."

Sun caressed the powerful sequoia trunks. A breeze stirred sequoia fronds.

Three deer grazed, each taking a shift at popping her head up and checking for danger while the other two ate.

At the far side, a mountain lion paused between bushy sapling sequoias to check the deer, and then the men. Roosevelt shot the lion with an imaginary rifle.

Muir was clearly irritated. "It's your natural reflex, isn't it?"

Roosevelt shrugged.

Muir pointed to one of the Guardians. "Do you understand this tree?"

Roosevelt looked up. "Understand that tree?"

Muir jumped off the porch, picked a wildflower, and stuck it into a buttonhole of Roosevelt's jacket. Roosevelt squirmed.

14
Sierra Forest
Twilight

Wa-Le-Co walked his Appaloosa quietly through the woods.

15
A Wild Man
Mariposa Grove - Twilight

Roosevelt wandered through the trees, which prevented any long view. He heard grunts and wild splashing, like wrestling in water. A warrior, Roosevelt sprinted forward to find Muir, nude, dancing in the river, sloshing himself.

"You are a wild man, John."

"You could pay me no greater compliment."

Roosevelt turned to leave.

"Care to bathe?" Muir invited.

"That water was snow an hour ago."

"Tiz a shock at first, but then gets mighty exhilarating."

"I leave you to your ablutions. You might be a hardier man than I."

Muir shook his head, "Now I've heard everything."

Roosevelt belly laughed and started to turn away again, but caught sight of Muir's calves.

The backs of Muir's legs were striped with scars, running parallel like tree rings, though slanted, from ankle to thigh.

Roosevelt winced. He trudged back to their camp, grave face. "The reality is worse than the rumors."[11]

16
Earth's
Tallest Glowing Candle
Sunset Tree - Night 1

Roosevelt and Muir sat near an Indian (small) fire, the light flickering across their faces. A tin coffee pot steamed next to the coals.

Roosevelt craned his neck to look toward the crown of the Sunset tree. They sat in lengthening shadows, but the top of the tree blazed from the setting sun like a giant candle. Roosevelt noted the fire scar 51 feet across its buttresses. "Amazing it can stand with such extensive damage."

"For 200 years," John said.

"200 years since fire caused that damage?" Roosevelt watched the earth's tallest glowing candle until it faded. "They have a presence."

"Yes, Sir. They are Beings. God has cared for these trees, saved them from drought, disease, avalanches, and a thousand straining, leveling tempests and floods; but he cannot save them from fools. They should be protected, these trees."

"They already are. By Abraham Lincoln, no less."

"You may be too confident. California is the

custodian. You were with the Governor of California today. Would you trust that blank-faced man with the well-being of this tree?"

Roosevelt said pointedly, "He's a good man. And my friend."

Muir lifted the tin pot from the fire. The President asked, "Home brew?"

"In a manner of speaking. Sequoia tea. I want to become more sequoiacal."

Roosevelt put his cup forward. "Will I become sequoiacal too?"

Muir splashed tea into Roosevelt's cup and said, sounding serious, "Couldn't hurt."

Roosevelt drank, spit it out.

John returned the pot to the coals with a small smile. He touched the bark of the tree near him. "Why do you suppose California is suffering from drought?"

"Not enough rain."

"The problem is not insufficient source, but insufficient retention." Muir jumped up. "Sequoias store water. Without them, rain too quickly finds community in joyful rivers, which perhaps flood, and then burble to the sea."

Near the rope corral, not far from the encampment and hidden by the trees, Wa-Le-Co watched the two men.

Muir paced to the Sunset Tree. He pointed south. "Once, the string of Sierra sequoias stretched for hundreds of miles—like a sponge, releasing trickles of water that lasted months, yielding vast flower gardens across the entire San Joaquin Valley."

Muir put his arm around the Sunset Tree, as if to comfort a friend. "Gone! Short-sighted greed is robbing California of its most important and scarce resource—water. When the drought comes, those dead monarchs could have saved 100 million crops."

"An ugly word is buried under your thesis, John."

As John sat, his expression conveyed a question.

"Restriction."

Muir's face hardened to defiance. Roosevelt, a man who knew men, watched.

"No, Sir! Preservation."

The two stared at each other, each firm in his perspective—total discord.

Roosevelt pulled back his energy. "Where'd you get your backbone, John?"

"Hard lesson: I shamed me-self, by not protecting me mither."

17
Romans 14:2-4
Wisconsin - 1851

John, a boy of 12, entered the kitchen of their two-story farmhouse in Central Wisconsin, his hair, arms, and hands wet from washing up.

Outside the door, the crops were about six inches high.

Dinner bubbled on the wood stove.

Ann, pregnant, sat at the table, sobbing into her arms, a letter clasped in her fist.

John rushed to her, gently pulled the letter free, and read it. "Gran—gone?" He asked plaintively.

John leaned over his mother, his arms around her, his head against her back, and cried with her. Her hand encircled his arm.

At suppertime, Ann bent over the stove, her face drawn.

Seven children sat at the well-scrubbed oak table with John. Margaret was the eldest at 16, then Sarah, 14, David, 10, Lad Daniel, 6, and twin girls, 4 years old.

Daniel Muir, military bearing, no-holds-barred tyrant, stalked in and sat at the head of the table. He pronounced, "We will no longer eat meat in this house."[12]

Ann bent over more, defeated, her burden increased.

John stood. "But Faither, Mither's--"

Daniel's voice held a warning. "Don't argue with me, Laddie. Vegetables, porridge, and only graham flour for bread."

John pled, "But, for now, Mither needs a lighter load. Her—"

"Genesis 1:29!"

John countered, "Romans 14:2-4."

All the older children tensed and drew themselves in. Ann turned, as if she had only just now understood what was going on. She froze, her mouth open.

Daniel crashed his chair backwards as he launched himself to stand over John, using his size to intimidate his son. He raised his voice, "Haud yer wheesht!"[13]

John cringed, glanced at his mother's back, and, shamefaced, sat.

By the time the furrows held half-grown crops, relentless summer sun had turned the soil dry and dusty. The heat scorched the children's backs as they weeded.

David, desperately thirsty, ran full into the creek at the corner of the field and splashed water into his mouth.

Daniel erupted from the house. "Out! Out of the creek! Back to work!" He broke a switch from a bush and advanced on David. The lad, wide-eyed, scared, sped to his dropped hoe.

Daniel watched while David forced himself to hoe harder, then the father returned to the house.

At end of day, the children sat at the table, their heads propped on their fists, eating their bread and vegetables listlessly.

Advancing thunder escorted heavy rain.

Daniel pointed. "John, go find the sheep and bring them in."

John left his meal and dashed into the downpour.

With the storm, night fell quickly. Daniel closed the Bible and climbed the stairs.

Ann looked out the window. She sat. She went to the window. She sat.

John finally entered, soaked and shivering. Ann dried him with a towel, then wrapped him in blankets and sat him close to the fireplace.   She toasted bread for him and brought him tea.

The next day, John, sitting at the table, propped his head up.

His mother noticed, "John, you aren't eating."

"Not hungry." He took one sip of milk and put the cup down.

"Ye should stay in bed today. Ye're sick."

Daniel pronounced, "No. He works."

Ann turned to Daniel, barely holding herself silent. The children left hurriedly. John stumbled to the door.

Daniel sat in his chair and opened the Bible. Ann

stood at the door and watched John stagger, then fall among the sheaves.

18

The Lord Knew What Was Good to Eat

Wisconsin - 1851

The windows were dark with night. Ann stood over Daniel, who was in his chair with the Bible. "He is verra sick, Daniel. Please, go for the doctor."

Daniel was unconcerned. "The laddie will pull through. God and hard work are by far the best doctors."[14] Daniel stared coldly at Ann.

Ann got her shawl and wrapped herself as she headed for the door.

Daniel stood. "Do not think you can disobey me." He took a threatening step toward her.

She put a protective arm across her unborn baby. He took another step. She looked up toward the bedroom where her son lay. She looked down at her unborn child. She looked at Daniel. She was clearly not afraid for herself.

She was forced to choose between a living and an unborn child.[15]

Ann hung up her shawl, defeated.

When the crops reached their full size, John returned to the table, where the family ate their usual sparse breakfast.

John stood. Still weak from hunger and sickness, he leaned straight-armed on the table to prop himself up. "Faither. We need to eat flesh. We cannot work as much as need be this hungry. The bairns greet from hunger."

Daniel took a bite of bread. "Eating flesh is foolish."

John asked, "Then why was Elijah fed meat by the ravens?"[16]

Daniel was silent. The family watched breathlessly. Daniel surged to his feet, knocking the chair over, and snatched his musket. The children froze. Daniel stared at John.

Ann, fearful that her husband would shoot her son, shrieked, "Nay, Daniel!"

Daniel stomped outside. Ann stepped to the window and watched after him. She turned toward her children. "He's goin' to hunt."

The corner of Ann's mouth turned up and her eyes shone with love for John.

A Madonna smile of sacred love.

19
Backbone
Mariposa Grove - 1903

"Backbone indeed," nodded Roosevelt.

Muir, never one to court admiration for himself, squatted and fed logs to the fire. Roosevelt studied him, not used to a man who wouldn't claim flattery and ride it like a horse for several miles.

"Hard it is to stand against a bully."

"A bully," said John, thoughtfully.

The campfire crackled. The men stared into the flames. Roosevelt, after a time, added, "You built a clock. How did you get the parts? In Wisconsin? It was wilderness then, I imagine. And this was—1850s?"

Muir answered easily, "I whittled the parts out of hickory."

Roosevelt raised his eyebrows. "I wanted to learn to fish, so I carved a mold, poured molten metal into it for a hook—"

John looked up, his eyes alight.

"—made cordage for a line, right after I felled a tree and burned a hollow into it to make a canoe."

John caught on. They laughed.

Roosevelt added, "I can't picture that your father would afford you time away from the plow for, I'm guessing now, a frivolous pursuit in his eyes."

"You're starting to know my father."

Roosevelt gave him a narrow-eyed look. "I've known lots of bullies. I'm in politics."

Muir repeated, "A bully."

"You've never used that word for him, have you?"

Muir shook his head. "My father made mistakes, I'll grant ye that—"

Roosevelt raised his brows and made a face, like, yeah a mistake.

John caught the expression, interpreted it accurately, and thought while the fire crackled. "You are quite an observer of men."

"I use more than one lens," Roosevelt said pointedly.

Roosevelt stood and made a pile of the remaining logs. "John, I don't mean to bring up a sensitive issue, but I couldn't help noticing the scars on your legs."

"My father's zeal for the Bible. He beat me everyday from the time I was a small boy. He was sure I must have done something wrong and he intended to beat the divil outa me."

Roosevelt's face showed his opinion—disgust at such a man. "You knew well then, what you risked, when you opposed him."

Muir looked deep into the fire while Roosevelt studied him.

"Must have been easy to leave the farm."

"Hard." John grabbed a long, bare branch and

tapped the earth. "Stayed longer than I wanted, to protect me mither and the bairns."

"You were their shield, weren't you? While he focused on you, they were safe."

Muir beat the ground with the stick.

"Something changed," perceived the astute President.

20

Rightful Ownership of Soil
Wisconsin - 1860

Daniel and George Mair, neighbor, fellow Scot, and farmer, chatted outside the barn as they watched the children working the field. Daniel leaned on a long-handled scythe.

The attention of both men was caught by an Indian man running through the distant woods.[17] Mair nodded in that direction. "I hate seeing those unfortunate natives pushed out of their own lands."

Daniel said authoritatively, "It could never have been God's intention to let those—aborigines—waste fertile country that Scotch and Irish farmers could make fruitful."

John stepped from the barn. In his 20s, John had wild red hair, tough and wiry muscle. John gestured toward the Indian. "Should not those who love land best have charge of it?"

Father and son glared at each other. John stood steadfast. "No thought to the welfare of the other fellow if he be weaker, eh Faither?"

Mair nodded and pointed at John in agreement.

His father spat, "Nature menaces man."

John said calmly, "Man menaces nature."

Ann stepped out of the creamery and calmly walked to stand between Daniel and John.

John immediately moved to guard his mother as Daniel stepped forward, his face mean.

Mair watched, eyes narrowed.

"They should take who have the power and they should keep who can."

"In what verse of the Old Testament will we find that, Faither?

Daniel stomped toward John. Ann stepped around John, to face Daniel.

John put his arms around his mother and swept her behind him, so that he was facing Daniel.

Ann panicked. She screamed, "First Timothy 3:3. No striker. Patient. The father is Not to STRIKE his weans!"

Daniel's face swelled with red rage. Ann struggled to get between John and Daniel. Sarah flew from the milk shed, skidded to a halt, and covered her mouth, terrified.

Daniel charged Ann as he lifted the scythe. Mair made a Scottish sound of alarm in his throat. He stepped toward them.

John twirled his mother easily, out of Daniel's way, releasing her toward Sarah, who grabbed Ann and pulled her into the shed. Sarah held the door closed and both women watched through the windows.

Daniel halted in front of John, scythe held like a bat.

John straightened his spine, stayed put. He shone

with inner fiber.

Daniel changed course and entered the barn as if he were busy.

Ann ran out and collapsed against John's side. He kissed her cheek. "Verra braw, Mither."

"Me!"

21
Tact
1903

"Backbone," pronounced Roosevelt, again.

"I saw I was endangering me mither by staying. She'd stand between us and he'd eventually hurt her."

Roosevelt studied John. "That's courage, John. You challenged an armed man who had governed his entire life on a self-aggrandizing philosophy."

John thought.

"No wonder you could turn me down when I asked you to be my guide. Your own compass is true."

A sound of rustling and hoof beats caused both men to leap to their feet. "Who knows we're here?" asked Roosevelt.

"Ever'body in the wide world."

They ran through the woods to the rope corral where the mules were tethered. John made a quick assessment. "Your mule is gone." He picked up the loose rope end that had held Roosevelt's mule.

The men fanned out into the forest. Each man searched separately through darkness, spooky.

At the edge of a small clearing, hiding next to the grazing mule, Wa-Le-Co held a branch aloft.

John entered the clearing and stepped toward the

mule.   He grabbed the mule's halter. Wa-Le-Co began to swing.

"I've got the mule."

"John?"

Wa-Le-Co froze. Roosevelt appeared from around a tree. Leidig ran up. John turned toward the corral. "I'll take him. I thought a cavalryman would tie better knots."

He led the mule back. Leidig and Roosevelt followed behind him.

Roosevelt said, "He doesn't seem familiar with tact."

Leidig answered, "Only when carpentering."

Roosevelt laughed, then checked Leidig sideways, unsure if the ranger was clever or ignorant.

22
Disagreement
May 16, 1903

At dawn, faint footsteps approached Roosevelt, asleep in his blankets. John poked Roosevelt with a stick. Roosevelt, the warrior, awakened instantly.

Muir put his finger to his lips. Muir and Roosevelt crept silently away from camp. The other men were still asleep.

John led Roosevelt down the trail next to the river. They came to the stage road.

"We go left, hot breakfast. Showers."

"We go right, no grasping dignitaries, no politics, and no endless petitions."

John could sympathize. What was a shower compared to peace?

They rode their mules across the bridge of the South Fork of the Merced. Soon they came to a trail leading upwards to the Northwest, heading away from the stage road.

Muir slowed his mule. "We stay on the stage road, we come to the main trail to Glacier Point. Easiest route."

Roosevelt used his chin to point right. "Where does that take us?"

"Cross country to Glacier Point—dangerous in spots,

and steep."

Roosevelt slapped his fist into his palm twice, then pointed right. "You understand I'm a hunter and a woodsman."

"You see the woods as an obstacle course with challenges for your manly sport."

"I also see the woods as a source of many essentials for the survival of a populace."

"To be exploited. To protect the economy of men already wealthy."

Roosevelt's face got tight. He chin-pointed. "That trail."

"Might be some bears."

Roosevelt pulled a folded Burgess rifle from his jacket pocket. Muir was shocked. "You can't shoot a bear in a National Park!"

"This sequoia woods is a State Park."

Muir nudged his mule onto the trail to the right, angry. "I'm stuck with a highhanded bushwhacker for three days."

Roosevelt nudged his mule to follow, looked amused. "If I cared about being popular, I wouldn't be President."

23
Sierra Forest

Wa-Le-Co studied the ground. He stepped one way, stopped, studied the ground, turned, headed another way, stopped, studied the ground.

He mounted the Appaloosa, nudged her forward, and leaned over the saddle to study the ground.

The rifle was in the scabbard.

24
Differences in Perspective
Upward Trail

The trail went upward, through woods. Roosevelt's jacket had wilting flowers in every buttonhole.

"Why did you leave the university without a degree?"

Muir answered, sending a twinkling glance sideways. "I got seduced." He enjoyed Roosevelt's reaction.

They entered a meadow sided by a rise toward a thickly forested ridge. Parallel to the bottom of the tree-line was a salmonberry thicket, waist-high on the bear foraging in it.

Muir noted movement on either side of the bear. A small snout poked up just above the foliage. Muir smiled.

Roosevelt clicked the rifle straight and aimed at the bear. Muir, so sharply interrupted in his joy at sight of the cub, spun his head a fraction after Roosevelt started to pull the trigger. "No!"

25
Sierra Forest

GUNSHOT!

Wa-Le-Co halted his horse. He looked in the direction of the shot and kicked his horse eastward through the woods.

26
Protector - Age 65
Sierra Trail

John grabbed the rifle. He and Roosevelt wrestled it back and forth.

The bear bolted from the thicket. Two cubs also galloped out. The mother bear and one cub ran to the left, west. The other panicked cub ran to the right, east.

Muir jerked the gun away. Roosevelt spurred his mule. It jumped into a full canter, toward the east.

Muir kicked his mule forward. He followed Roosevelt through the woods.

A metal and glass compass hung from Roosevelt's belt, swinging wildly. The glass face shattered. Water drops flung out.

Muir, hanging on, took his bearings. The expression on his face showed strong fear. "Sir! Mr. President! Colonel! Stop!"

Roosevelt's mule gained speed.

Muir yelled, "Watch out! Cliff!"

Roosevelt's mule popped out of the woods. The trail bent toward a perilous section too near a sheer cliff. Muir followed.

Wa-Le-Co, on the Appaloosa, emerged from the woods some distance behind Muir. He immediately took in the situation, slowed his horse to a stop, and watched.

Roosevelt saw the danger, and tried to slow the mule. The mule was panicked and not responding. Roosevelt eyed the cliff-edge ahead, leaned and pressed knees to get the mule to turn. The mule kept charging. The trail now verged alongside the cliff.

Roosevelt showed true fear.

Muir cantered his mule to the outside of Roosevelt's mule— bringing himself dangerously close to the drop —and herded the darker mule into the forest, away from the canyon.

Wa-Le-Co stared after the vanished men, thinking. He seemed to be going deep inside. He looked up to the sky, then clucked the Appaloosa back into the woods.

Holding the other halter, Muir led Roosevelt and the mule deeper into the forest. Muir waved his arm in angry, jerky gestures. "You would shoot an innocent beast? And risk your mule? Automatically? For no reason?"

Both men panted Muir jumped down from the saddle, mad as a wasp. He shook his head while he tied his mule to a tree. He ran his hands down its legs, still grumbling.

Roosevelt said, "It's my mule that you're worried about." He slid down from the saddle, shaky. He tied his mule.

Muir spat, "Mule did'nae have a choice."

Roosevelt halted a fraction of a second to look at Muir, then stepped to the mule's head and stroked the animal, making soothing sounds.

John's volume dropped one tenth of a bell. "I look an animal in the face and I see a cousin, or an aunt."

Roosevelt, voice still at his previous loud decibel, shouted, "You were a farmer!"

"Yes, taking creatures to feed my family. You would deprive bear cubs of their protection. Why?" He recovered that lost decibel. "To stick their mama's head on a wall? To boast at your pricey club?"

Roosevelt looked around. "What cubs?"

John rammed his fists into his thighs, facing Roosevelt head on. "How would a fixed, glass-eyed head compare to her noble, intelligent face as she teaches her cubs to eat?"

Roosevelt, a boxer, curled his hands into fists. "I'd never take a mama bear."

Muir turned away and stroked the mule's neck, soothing himself as much as it. "Indeed you would have —just now—had I nae stopped ye."

Muir stood straight and righteous. "And is that no the difference between us? You would shoot, automatically, not fully comprehending the situation. To you, that bear, and this woods—just objects—to be used."

He gestured to the forest surrounding them, shouting again, "And, for your information, this is Yosemite

National Park—No Hunting!"

His anger rekindled, Muir turned and gestured to include the entire planet. "Do you think this whole world is just for the enjoyment of man? To plunder and use whatever he wants?"

Muir glared at Roosevelt, waiting for him to answer.

The President glared back, waiting for an apology. "I'm used to insults by people who are clawing their own staircase over my skin." Roosevelt added, almost a prompt, "I am no longer accustomed to men speaking plainly to me out of personal disinterest."

Muir, who would never consider plain speaking an offense, was silent.

"I have no idea where I am, or how I would get back. My people do not know where I am. None of them know this wilderness."

"Not many do," affirmed Muir. "Do you want to go back? You can put all those people back on your shoulders."

"You have kidnapped me."

"Why worry? I don't kill things." He paused, and added shouting, "Mr. Teddy Bear!" Muir stomped off. Roosevelt growled like a bear.

The lone bear cub stopped running. And looked around. He discovered he was alone.

27
Orders Versus Commission
Wawona Big Trees Hotel

Zach, pistol in holster, paced on the veranda. He occasionally paused to peer up the wagon road. Elias came out, put on his hat and watched him. Zach headed for the barn. He grabbed his saddle and headed toward his horse.

"What are you doing, Zach?"

"Gonna find the President."

"What could hurt him here? 750,000 acres of nothing."

Zach saddled and bridled his horse.

"You will defy orders?"

"Elias, we are the first, the very first, full-time Secret Service agents."

"I know."

Zach led his horse from the barn. "After McKinley was shot, Treasury figgered losing three Presidents kinda looked bad." He handed the reins to Elias. "We are forging this job. And our orders from our superior officer are to protect the President—full time."

Zach ran up the steps and into the hotel.

Elias shouted after him, "The President ordered us *here*."

Moments later Zach returned with a pack and

canteen. He attached these to his saddle, mounted.

Elias looked up at him. "*He* is Commander-in-*Chief. The* superior officer."

Zach turned his horse down toward the Valley Trail. Elias slammed his hat onto the road.

28
Why Worry?
Sierra Forest

"Why worry? I'm alone in a wilderness with a hot-headed Scot—" Roosevelt pulled a round from his pocket. "—And only a single bullet."

He took the rifle from Muir's mule and loaded it.

29
Swale

Wa-Le-Co walked his horse slowly, listening to Roosevelt yelling in the distance.

"I'm the President of the United States!"

Wa-Le-Co slid off his horse, tied it, grabbed his rifle, and crept toward the President's voice.

30
Lost
Sierra Forest

Roosevelt ripped the wildflowers from his buttonholes. He marched back the way they had come, rifle in hand. The forest closed-up around him.

He slowed. No trail. He looked back. No mule.

The bear cub, distracted by a berry bush, foraged beyond Roosevelt. As the man passed, the cub lifted his head and made a soft cub grunt.

Westerly, the mother bear lifted her head and turned around.

Roosevelt pulled a map from his pocket, looked, swiveled. Filtered by the trees, the sun, now close to overhead, gave little hint as to direction. The trees themselves created a sameness of view in all directions.

To a man used to being the most powerful person in any situation—even as an experienced hunter, nearly always surrounded by guides, carriers, cooks, servants, and toadying companions—this was a unique experience.

He had absolutely no power over anything here.

He studied the map. "The whole Park reduced to this one page. Useless. Fortunately, I have modern technology." He pulled the compass from his belt—

broken. Roosevelt put the map back in his pocket.

He stomped far enough in one direction to come to the edge of a sheer cliff. Was this the same cliff or a different cliff? In his earlier panicked ride, he could not have put any attention on contextual hints.

He pivoted and stomped more cautiously in the other direction.

Theodore Roosevelt stopped. His face lost all arrogance. He swiveled slowly—endless trees in every direction. He was just a man, in a strange forest, alone. President didn't count here.

A large beast crashed through the woods, coming closer. Roosevelt backed up, concerned.

Wa-Le-Co watched from behind a tree.

The crashing came closer. Roosevelt ran.

Wa-Le-Co shook his head. Big mistake.

The mama bear chased Roosevelt, looking 10 feet high and as if her claws were a foot long.

Roosevelt yelled, "Mr. Muir! John!"

Running steps thudded toward them.

Wa-Le-Co turned swiftly to face the approaching man. He aimed his rifle with deadly focus.

Muir loped into sight. He unknowingly veered behind Wa-Le-Co as he hastened toward Roosevelt, who was backing up, with his rifle aimed toward the bear.

Roosevelt's heel caught the edge of a submerged granite slab and he fell, dropping the rifle. The mama

bear was getting closer. Muir snatched up the rifle,
turned to face the charging bear.

31
Unshod Prints

Junction of Wawona Road & Glacier Point Trail

Zach, riding at the side of the down-sloping trail, halted. He pointed to the north, the direction they traveled. "If we continue this way, we'll go down to Yosemite Valley." He pointed east. "That's the trail to Glacier Point, where they are supposed to camp tonight." Zach turned his horse to look back up the way they had just come. "Muir and Roosevelt did not come this way, although this would be the most usual and gradual route."

"How do you know?"

Zach pointed to the fairly smooth, wind-blown trail. "No mule prints." Zach bent over from his saddle and studied the ground. "But horse prints, unshod, come up-slope from the Valley."

Zach turned his horse and looked upslope. "That horse went toward Wawona, but not long ago, came back." Zach looked downslope. "And didn't continue on to the Valley."

Zach clucked his horse onto the side trail, peered ahead. "No prints here. Uh-oh. The horse's prints pick up further down the Glacier point trail."

"So what?"

"An unshod horse. Indian!"

"But you said no mule prints. So this guy doesn't know where they are either."

"He's an Indian, Elias. He can track better than we can."

"Why would an Indian be after the President?"

"Removing Indians from their native lands? Jailing them for protecting their children? Elias, do you pay any attention to—never mind." Zach walked his horse further onto the Glacier Point trail. He gave Elias a firm look.

Elias looked stubborn.

"Elias, we are here to protect the President's ass."

"He's riding a mule."

Distant *GUNSHOT!*

32
A Full-Fledged Man
Sierra Forest

The bear cub jumped to cling to a tree past Wa-Le-Co. Muir threw down the shotgun like it was poison.

The mother bear changed course, running now directly toward—Wa-Le-Co, who quickly stood with his arms overhead, making himself look as big as possible. He backed slowly, away from the beeline between Mama and cub.

The crashing sound stopped. Bear grunting was answered by cub purring. The little family sorted itself out.

Muir listened, smiled, then looked down at Roosevelt, who was groping around blindly.

"My spectacles fell off."

Muir saw the glasses lying on a tussock. He picked them up and put them in his pocket.

"Give those to me."

"No."

"Then the camping trip is over. Can't see an elephant without them."

"Trade you the spectacles for the rifle."

"I'm the President of the United States."

"Thus it's my duty as a citizen to help you not commit

a felony."

Roosevelt handed the shotgun to Muir. "You are a completely different kind of man than I'm used to."

"That I believe. I just can't decide if that's a compliment or an insult—to your way of thinking."

Roosevelt laughed out of sheer relief.

John asked, "Are you ready to see now?" He handed the glasses to Roosevelt.

The President, a different man himself than he was 30 minutes ago, looked up as he put them on. Over his head, the brilliant blue feather of a stellar jay—held by the thread of a spider web—was caught midair in a ray of sun.

When one has just survived death, life itself has a sweetness and simplicity as if one is brand new. Roosevelt reached for the feather as the gift it was.

Muir led unerringly, without hesitation, through the featureless forest toward the mules. "But if you got eaten by a bear, that would only be sporting, right?"

Roosevelt graciously said, "I admit to the thrill of the hunt, the skill of the eye, the coordination with the weapon."

They walked, not looking at each other, but Muir listened keenly.

"What you say is part of it also, probably what made me angry. I was a sickly child. Asthma. I discovered that if I pushed myself—climbed mountains, hiked—my asthma went away. But I still couldn't do what other boys did. Clumsy. Not coordinated. I couldn't shoot a barn much less a target. And then I realized others could see what I couldn't. And my father got me spectacles, and suddenly this elaborate world appeared."

Muir nodded, understanding.

"So I've been catching up. Hunting is part of that."

Muir turned to the President, "I think you have caught up, Sir. I have certainty that achieving the Presidency is proof of your status as a full fledged man."

Roosevelt guffawed, bent over, hands on knees. Muir joined.

33
Destinies of Men Determined
Sierra Forest - 1903

John sauntered, his usual pace, and the President, used to striding manfully, did John the very great honor of adjusting to his more relaxed gait.

"You left the University without a degree, because you were seduced? By a woman?"

"Locust tree."

"I hear that all the time."

"A passing friend had a locust branch, and he opened a door to my future. It was just at the end of the Civil War, and a hospital tent was near the University."

Roosevelt sat on a boulder.

"I would read the Bible to the wounded soldiers, or write letters, or pray with them."

Roosevelt's face filled with a beautiful respect.

"It wasn't enough, so I applied to medical school."

"You know I'm a soldier, John, more than I'm anything else. And I can tell you—that was everything to those boys."

"They *were* boys. But I never heard back about my application. And the classroom started to seem irrelevant."

Both men looked down, in sorrow, and remembrance.

"That locust leaf—it opened my new path."

Roosevelt said drily, "I understand totally. Now you've discovered my secret vice. I'd lose all my senses if someone thrust a locust twig toward me."

Muir guffawed. "I tasted that leaf."

"Nothing like a good meal of locust leaves."

"So, Colonel Wise-apple, what did that leaf taste like?"

Roosevelt shook his head, "No idea."

"A garden pea."

Roosevelt shrugged, "I admit it. I'm not comprehending how this would be earth shattering."

"The tree tasted like the vegetable!"

Roosevelt nodded his head slowly. "Well, that would change my life too." He jumped up.

Muir shoved his fists into his hips, as if to underline how obvious was his point. "That sturdy tree and the delicate viney plant—they are relatives. I felt lightning-struck."

Roosevelt looked innocent, "I feel that way now."

John eyed him.

Roosevelt spread both palms up, as if weighing two things. "Education. Garden pea. You would absolutely have to abandon college."

They both laughed, and resumed walking.

"I see you have no discovered the wonders of

botanizing."

"I never thought it essential when it came to governing men."

"And there, Sir, you may have missed a life lesson. Some of my best friends are plants."

"Strangely, that I can understand." Roosevelt dodged a boulder. "From such chance encounters are the destinies of men determined."[18]

The sky was a clear lake-bottom blue. The men strode together. "So then you walked to Cuba?"

"By way of Canada."

"Yes, Canada is conveniently on the way to Cuba from Wisconsin."

"I wanted to find a wee orchid."

"If I had a penny for every time I heard that—"

"You'd have one penny. Two if you knew Jeanne Carr."

Muir and Roosevelt walked on rounded granite boulder tops, the bulk of the boulders submerged. Muir leaned over to study the granite. Roosevelt looked too.

"Jeanne Carr?"

"Wisconsin Professor's wife. My most faithful pen-friend."

"I heard that you lost your eyesight in Indianapolis, but you didn't give up."

"I had a bad moment." The two men turned toward each other. "Did you ever feel that every single thing of value to you was lost?"

Into Roosevelt's mind jumped the sight of his beloved ranch in the Dakotas, cinders. And on the range, his carefully bred cattle, frozen. "And for maybe a moment, you don't see how to go on?"

"Aye."

Both men looked grave, both remembering.

"But a Specialist said my sight would return in the one eye and the other might partly recover. And Mrs. Carr, who had handed me from one stepping stone to the next, sent me flowers and the *California Magazine*."

Muir turned a different direction and leapt from one granite top to three others in a row—a giant's stepping stones. Roosevelt, heftier, wound himself up to make the same leaps.

Muir entered thickly placed trees. Roosevelt pivoted 360 degrees—to see no discernible landmark and no trail—then followed.

"Every fork in my road, she has sensed my soul's direction."

Roosevelt panted lightly. "That magazine —your first exposure to Yosemite?"

"Second. I had heard about Yosemite earlier. And it haunted me. Then, with that article, a magnet in my body started tugging on me."

Roosevelt sat on a bench-high boulder. He pulled sandwiches from his pocket, handed Muir one. "What flowers did Mrs. Carr send?"

"Hepaticas and violets."

Roosevelt raised his sandwich to his mouth, then dropped his arm without taking a bite. "Hepaticas and violets? You know each flower has a meaning? She was sending you a message, John."

"Aye. That I still had plants to live for."

Roosevelt shrugged, bit into his sandwich. "Your sight came back and you headed south. You were in your 20s?"

"I was scared my vision was fleeting. I wanted to see tropical flora while I still could."

"So you walked to—"

"Florida, Cedar Key. And on the way, I began to understand that my father's interpretation of the Bible had to be incorrect."

"What do you mean?"

34
Attacked!

Scottish Lowland Meadow
Dunbar, Scotland - 1843

Wee John, 5 years of age, sat cross-legged as still as a stone, in a rolling meadow. He gazed at one heather bloom, amid raspberry-pink clusters of tiny blooms that carpeted the meadow.

His expression—pure joy. Remarkable focus for a 5-year-old.

Three bigger lads, maybe 10-13 years-old, crept toward John. They looked mean.

John was too absorbed to notice the boys as they slinked closer. When they attacked John, they got in some hard hits before John could muster a defense.

35
Protector - Age 5
Muir Home
Dunbar, Scotland - 1843

On the main street of the seaside town was a broad three-story brown-stone building. "Daniel Muir - Meal" was painted on the ground-floor windows.

The family home began on the second floor. It was a combination of well off—in the sense of sturdy well-made furniture, thick rug, abundant wood for the fire, and stark—no pictures or decorations, no conveniences for Ann, such as a stove, or more than one truly comfortable chair.

Ann Muir, 27, pregnant, bent over pots on grates and cranes in a fireplace.

She straightened slowly, smoothed one hand over her full belly, and pressed the other hand into the crook of her back.

Ann's eyes rested on an empty chair at a well-scrubbed oak table and then darted to her husband. She blew out a worried breath.

Daniel Muir, in his 30s, sat in the sole comfortable chair, reading the Bible. He glanced often at the back stairwell and the empty chair at the table, increasingly irritated.

Three children read at the table. Margaret, 9, and Sarah, 7, shared a Bible. Margaret lifted her eyes to the empty chair and then peered out the back window as if she could see to the seaside tide pool or stand of trees or flowered meadow that had snared her brother.

David, 3, had his hand on an open Bible that lay between him and the empty chair. He lifted his eyes to share a worried glance with Sarah.

With a stomp on the wooden stairs from below, Ann looked relieved, but her worry returned. The stomp was from a man's weight, and an extra tap indicated a cane.

The children all looked up, identified the stomp, smiled, and looked toward the head of the stairs. Their grandfather, David Gilrye, in his 60's, comfortable family-man, tottered in.

"Gran!" Wee David started to rise. Sarah reached over to hold him down, with a glance toward Daniel.

David read the room and circled the table, hugging each child from behind.

At the empty chair, he exchanged a look with Sarah, who head-pointed out the back window. David looked over at Daniel, shook his head.

Ann started to lift a heavy pot from the fire. David rushed, tottering, to help her.

"Hold, Lass. Let me help."

She bent backward, then gave him a doubtful smile. He wasn't so spry himself anymore.

Daniel called, still sitting. "I'm joining a different church, David."

"Are ye now."

"Campbell, he's the one adheres to the Word of the Lord."

"That mon!"

Ann shook her head.

"And are ye after another new religion now, Daniel Muir? Again. And is this to express yur love of the Almighty?"

Daniel's face reddened. He raised his fist.

Ann put her hand over her mouth, fearful. The children glanced nervously between their father and grandfather.

The back door slammed. Quick steps smacked up the stairs.

John limped in. His eye was turning black. Ann cried out, grabbed a wet cloth, and rushed toward him.

Daniel made a harsh Scottish sound of anger, leapt from the chair, and slammed his arm in front of Ann's pregnant belly. She stopped just in time to avoid being rammed. David gently pulled Ann away from Daniel.

"Ye have done bad things, John. Go cut a switch!"

Margaret stood. "But Faither. The big schoolboys attack the bairns all the time."

Daniel lunged to tower over Margaret. She backed up, then bravely took one step toward him.

When David shuffled to get between Margaret and

Daniel, John deliberately moved into his father's sight-line to pull his father's attention away from his sister and his grandfather.

"I'm ready, Faither."

Daniel shoved John toward the door.

Ann stepped forward. "Daniel. No! He's only 5. He would'nae do a bad thing."

Daniel fixed Ann with a savage glare. He turned toward her, menacingly.

Ann cupped her unborn child with her palms. David, though precarious, moved to stand in front of his daughter.

John again shifted into his father's sightline.

"Faither?"

Daniel yanked John down the stairs, as if John had been resisting him. From outside came the sound of flesh being struck.

Ann grabbed the back of a chair and bent over it like an old woman. David embraced her, and the children encircled them, the girls crying.

36
The Mark of Cain
Wisconsin Farm - 1849

Sandy scrub land surrounded a small, rough shanty.

Daniel, Sarah, 13, David, 9, and John, 11, tromped out to the field. It was their first day as farmers.

Daniel pointed John toward the heavy share plow, the handles of which were nearly over his head.

John awkwardly plowed a furrow to the end of the field. The furrow was wobbly, uneven. Daniel watched John with disapproval. John struggled to lift and turn the plow to make the next furrow.

Sarah and David chopped clods with hoes.

Daniel entered the shanty.

For a time, the children struggled with the unfamiliar work, then, as John next turned the plow, he noticed a snipe, struggling in the meadow beyond the field. John ran over to her.

Sarah called, her voice low, "John! Back to the plow!"

He studied the bird. "Her egg is stuck. It's too heavy for her to lift herself to get the leverage to release it."

Nervous, Sarah glanced between the shanty and John, who sat beside the bird and gently picked her up.

From inside the shanty, they could hear a chair scrape against the wooden floor.

Sarah hissed, "John! Faither!"

"How can I abandon her? Her heartbeat is rat-a-tating into me hands."

Sarah whispered, "David!"

He lifted his eyes. Sarah head-pointed him to move closer to her.

Daniel's footsteps stomped closer to the door of the shanty.

Sarah and David lined themselves up to block view of John. John gently freed the egg from the bird. She flew up to a branch.

The screen door screeched.

That night, the boys, hair wet, faces scrubbed, sat at the small table with Bibles while Sarah cooked.

John said, "Our Scots neighbor, Mr. Mair, says that slavery is evil."

Daniel rose from his chair and clomped to the plain table. He towered over John. "Nay, it is not."

John's shoulders tightened and drew in.

Daniel said forcibly, "The New Testament does not condemn it." He sat. His tone more reasonable, he added, "When Alexander Campbell came to Scotland, he preached that slavery is moral. The races are not equal. Some bear the Mark of Cain."

"What is the mark of Cain, Faither?"

"Dark skin."

"Dark skin? But there are no such people here. How

will you preach to them?"

"It also means those who live as fugitives from a right and proper life. The unclean. Such heathens are here aplenty."

"The unclean are heathen? And Jacob said, 'Be clean.'"

Daniel's face became slightly less harsh. John's shoulders relaxed. Sarah set bowls of stew before the males.

As they finished their stew, John asked, "Why did we come to America, Faither?"

"I am called to convert those heathens. We obey God by following the concrete facts of the Bible, not gauzy abstractions or philosophies."

"Would that not be a philosophy?"

Sarah tensed. David put his hand to his forehead and closed his eyes.

"Are ye trying to test me, John? It is my duty to spread the gospel to heathens. The destiny of the whole world depends on the Anglo Saxon race."

John absorbed this message.

37
Unyoking from a Father's View
Rolling Fork Stream
Kentucky - 1867

John, 29, came to a wide mountain stream, rapids foaming around boulders of various sizes. On his back was a wooden plant press and a heavy-looking knapsack. He carried a stripped tree branch as a walking stick.

The creek had deep holes with swirling currents and uncertain bottom, not visible under the foam. John poked the stick into the rapids and then stepped into them.

After another two steps, the stick was ripped from his hand and carried swiftly away. With his next step, his leg sank deep and he swayed, off balance. He waved his arms, trying to not fall.

John turned back toward the bank, but when he stepped, the force of the water nearly pushed him over. He struggled. He was in trouble.

Mae, a skeletal black woman in her 70s, ran up to the opposite bank. Her arms were stretched forward, palms upright.

"Wait! Mistuh, wait! Or sartain you be killed."

"The water didn't appear to be deep."

"No one ever wade that river." Mae scurried off toward an old homestead. She called, "Abe! Bring the ferry horse!"

She returned, ahead of a white horse with Abe, a small black boy clinging to its back.

Horse and boy made a tottering, halting crossing. John scrambled up behind the boy. The horse rocked and stumbled as it turned, nearly falling, but Abe steadied it and they crossed to the other side.

John slid off the horse, swayed. Mae steadied him, then led him to the house. John followed, looking at the large, open home and the virtual town of small shacks for the black workers.

Mae motioned John to a rocker on the porch. He sank into it gratefully. A blacksmith with worn, singed clothes stepped up on the porch and settled with a sigh onto the next rocker.

"Where you be headed, Mistuh?"

"Venezuela."

"That in Georgia?"

"South America."

Mae brought them water and johnny cakes.

"Thank ye, Miz Mae."

She handed John the cup of water as the blacksmith warned, "The war may be over, Mistuh, but these mountains be not safe. Brigands still ambush lone travelers."

"I'm a lover of trees and flowers. Want to meet as many as I can."

Mae nodded, "You got gumption."

"Gumption." John tested the word. Tasted it. Liked it. "Gumption."

When he'd recovered, he thanked the two good people of the settlement, and went on his way. As he sauntered alongside a mutilated train track, a carter, a black man driving a team of oxen, overtook him. The wagon held barrels of produce.

The carter pulled the reins. "Whoa. Wanta ride, Suh?"

John doffed his hat and climbed up into the wagon. "John Muir."

"Mistuh Carter." Carter pointed to the ruined train track. "Right heah is where Rebs was a-pullin' up the track. And they thought they seed the Yankees a-comin, and L'od how they run."[19]

"They were making you pull up track too. Which is how you witnessed this."

Carter nodded.

"And you did not run, because you were not in danger from the Yankees." Muir turned shrewd regard toward Carter. "Must have been a pleasant change to see those white overseers rabbiting through the woods."

Carter peeked at Muir with surprise, not expecting a

white man to have that kind of perception. "Didn't make me sad, Suh."

They shared a laugh.

38
Thinking Wider
Yosemite Wilderness - May 16, 1903

John and Roosevelt both sat on boulders and ate their sandwiches. "Knowing now, the cruel hardships that people endured, I wonder at their kindnesses toward me."

Roosevelt brushed crumbs off his hands as John stood. "My only knowledge of Africans had been from my faither." John headed on through the woods. "That ramble started me thinking wider."

"Thinking wider?" Roosevelt followed.

"Many of those Kentucky negroes were shrewd and intelligent, and when warmed upon a subject that interested them, eloquent in no mean degree."

Muir picked up a sugar pine cone and eyed Roosevelt's jacket as if he were trying to figure out how to attach the enormous cone. Roosevelt laughed, then took the cone and studied it as they walked.

"Mark of Cain!" John reasoned, "What God of Love would condemn an entire race for one ancestor's mistake?"

"Still, white men from European stock are superior."

"Are they? As a lad, I held no separate view from my father's. And like my father, unthinkingly, I called them sambos and sallies."

Muir leading, they popped out of the woods to see El Capitan—enormous, riveting. Roosevelt took a huge gasping breath.

"But the real, actual individuals started chiseling away at my inherited point of view."

"The majority of Southern Negroes are unfit for suffrage," insisted Roosevelt.

"In the South, I found—when I would talk to a Negro individual—sound opinions, a knowledge of agriculture, a loyalty to family."

Muir scrambled, like a mountain goat, down a slope alongside a white, frothy cascade. Roosevelt, hanging on to branches and stumbling and grumbling, followed. At the base, he bent over, hands on knees, panting. "Will we ever find anything to agree on, John?"

"How about this?"

When Roosevelt straightened, he faced Yosemite, from above the west opening of the Valley— breathtaking, vast, unworldly, exquisite. Roosevelt fell back to sit on a boulder.

John laughed. "Your legs lost their gumption. Same thing happened when I first saw this Valley."

Both men stared silently.

39
7000' Elevation
Granite Stepping Stones

Wa-Le-Co slowly swiveled. Too much granite. No footprints.

40
6000′ Elevation
Sierra Forest

Elias sat his mule while Zach rode in a slow large circle, bending down from his saddle. Zach shook his head. "We still haven't crossed mule track."

"Or horse track, since the trailhead."

"This table-land is larger than it looks on a map. No idea how far we are from the President."

The men kicked their steeds into a canter. From overhead, the sides of the cliffs came closer.

A hawk got interested.

41
The Selfish Propriety of Civilized Man
Sierra Trail

John and Roosevelt came to a thicket of salmonberries. John plucked one and handed it to Roosevelt. He popped it into his mouth, trusting John.

An eagle soared overhead. Both men looked up. Roosevelt pointed an imaginary rifle and Muir shook his head, disgusted.

"Have you ever watched eagle parents teach their child to hunt? Destroying a magnificent creature—interrupting her own noble life—for superficial—"

Roosevelt's face tightened in anger. Muir saw, and continued anyway, "Aye, for superficial reasons—for status or bragging rights or even for coming-of-age rituals—unless that entire animal is needed for survival of a family or a tribe." They glared at each other. "That is wanton, unconscious slaughter."

John marched on, waving his arms. Roosevelt marched behind. "Aye, unconscious. Not thinking—about the animal. The animal's life. The animal's equal birthright."

By now, they had re-accessed elevation and could

see down into the Valley from the cliffside trail. Muir waved his arm downward. "The Ahwahneechee. Who inhabited this Valley. Until greed drove them out. Used ever' scrap of any animal they took. No waste of a breathing creature. Honored as spiritual brethren."

He turned to face Roosevelt head on. "I have never yet happened on a trace of evidence...that any one animal was ever made for another as much as it was made for itself."

John stomped on. Roosevelt stomped after him. "I suppose if a snake slithered over your foot, you'd say, 'Mornin' Uncle.'"

John paused just long enough for Roosevelt to catch up. "Though alligators, snakes, naturally repel us, they are not mysterious evils. They are part of God's family, unfallen, undepraved, and cared for with the same species of tenderness and love as is bestowed on angels in heaven or saints on earth."

Muir's entire concept startled President.Roosevelt. Muir continued, "I think that most of the antipathies which haunt and terrify us are morbid productions of ignorance and weakness. I have better thoughts of alligators now that I have seen them at home in the Everglades. Honorable representatives of the great saurians of an older creation."[20]

"And," Muir added, musing, "we can apply that principle to varieties of humankind as well. Let a Christian hunter go to the Lord's woods and kill his well-kept beasts, or his—the Lord's—wild Indians, and it is well; but let an enterprising specimen of these proper and—according to those who claim supremacy—predestined victims go to houses and fields and kill the most worthless person of the vertical godlike killers,—oh! that is horribly unorthodox, and on the part of the Indians atrocious murder! Well, I have precious little sympathy for the selfish propriety of civilized man, and if a war of races should occur between the wild beasts and Lord Man, I would be tempted to sympathize with the bears."[21]

Roosevelt pulled a map out of his pocket and spread it across a medium high boulder. "I saw that you've drawn a different boundary for the Park. Your proposal for the new Yosemite perimeter has an odd shape. Almost like an arrowhead. Why?"

"The watershed." Muir leaned over to trace rivers that flowed into the Valley. "I've re-drawn the boundary so that all headwaters of streams that flow into the valley would be inside it."[22]

"You walked the organic perimeter of the Park?" Roosevelt straightened, then added, "Of course."[23]

They arrived at the edge of another cliff, which hovered above the main Valley.

Yosemite Falls danced like a happy thing on the other side.

Muir whispered, "'In wildness is the preservation of the world.'"

Roosevelt cited, "Thoreau."

Muir turned, in all earnestness, toward Roosevelt. "When we rip the earth's fabric, we know not what we destroy, what future essential remedy we are killing in our ignorance."

"Like the sequoias, which store water."

John nodded, "If we do not respect the wilderness, we kill our children with our own hands."

Roosevelt countered, "Emerson says that things refuse to be mismanaged long."

Muir countered, "Except with regard to forests, which have been mismanaged rather long, and now come desperately near being like smashed eggs and spilt milk."[24]

Roosevelt studied Muir's face as Muir looked down at the Valley. "You love this land."

With naked devotion, Muir nodded, "More than my own life."

Roosevelt stepped forward to look down into the Valley, cleared his throat, and manfully tried to avoid weeping.

Muir bent to look into the face of a very plain flower on a very unattractive weed. He touched the stem lovingly. Then straightened. "Course by my faither's definition, I was a fugitive from a right and proper life—like the Indians—unclean. But I became certain that my work was for people to perceive that each natural entity has its own essential place and existence."

Roosevelt faced John. "You do know your father was wrong about you."

It was John's turn to be startled.

"It's by following your heart that you've had momentous effect."

Muir caressed a smooth boulder, like petting his dog, almost as if he were soothing himself at the thought of such a change in self-perspective. He sauntered on, either speechless or thoughtful.

Roosevelt pet the boulder, really looking at it. Then he shook his head, straightened, and hurried on after John.

At the mules, the men checked their tack.

42
Three Frogs
Rim of Yosemite Valley

Now mounted, John and Roosevelt walked their mules side-by-side. Muir pointed across the valley. "The Three Brothers, or, according to the Ahwahneechee, Pompomposus, which means, Three Frogs—uh, never mind."

John clucked his mule forward.

"Three Frogs—what?"

Roosevelt clucked his mule after John. John turned red in the face. "Having…relations."

"Three Frogs Fu—"

Roosevelt nearly fell off his mule laughing. Muir, still embarrassed, walked his mule ahead.

Roosevelt looked across Yosemite Valley. He could see the point of the native name. He laughed again. "John Muir. Touchy. Impatient. Inflexible. Wildly courageous—and a prude." He had a look of wonder. "I like the man."

Roosevelt caught up to John. "You wouldn't make it in politics."

"Thank the good Lord."

The trees thinned as they curved around the base of Sentinel Dome.

John said, "You don't seem worried about enemies."

"I have powerful enemies, it is true. But I also have powerful friends."

"That didn't keep McKinley from being assassinated."

"I won't let fear stop me."

"Neither did I."

Roosevelt abruptly turned his head toward John. "You still have powerful enemies, John."

"Whitney hated me. That is certain. But would not have taken physical action against me. And he's gone."

"Now, John. At this very moment."

Muir pulled his mule to a halt at the level area near the base of Sentinel Dome. He jumped down from the saddle.

Roosevelt continued, "Men intent upon profit can be ruthless. You see through their public palaver. And you stir opposition to their greedy pursuits."

John looked up at Roosevelt. "Someone has to stop mindless development." He tied his mule and removed the saddle. "I don't suppose any of those wealthy men —and you are an exception—looks ahead 10 years, 50 years, to see what their grasping leads to."

"John, take me seriously. You are in danger."

Muir focused on Roosevelt. He absorbed the reality of his peril. His face showed his sudden awareness that he was indeed a target and fear flashed across his face, but he pulled a brush from his saddle bag and brushed the damp hide of his mule.

"You truly discount the danger to yourself? Have you no fear?" asked the President.

"I do. I don't actually think much of my own mortality. But the thought of not being there for Louie and my daughters—" Muir walked the mule in a circle to dry him. Roosevelt watched. Muir tied the mule in a shaded place, then stepped to look over Yosemite Valley, down toward El Cap, across to Yosemite Falls.

"You propose that I leave this glorious Sierra unprotected?"

43
Everybody Needs Beauty
Between Sentinel Dome & Glacier Point
Twilight

John and Roosevelt built an Indian fire together, talking as—both woodsmen—they expertly added logs.

"So will you back off, now that you know your jeopardy is real? I don't mean with me, but in the face of opposition far more powerful—and dare I say, far less principled—than you?"

"I should creep backward and say, 'Here, take the forests that heal?'" Muir bowed as if to a king. "Go ahead, rich man. Continue to take more than you need, even though you are stealing the water from ten thousand farmers. Don't worry that your slaughter of predators will ruin the balance of forest or prairie."

Roosevelt slammed his fist twice into his palm. "That's it! That's exactly what I'm talking about. That attitude—absent all diplomacy—in your speeches, in your articles. You have enemies!"

"I'm simply not important enough."

The fire had a low flame. Each man roasted a steak.

"Nearly every man in my world exaggerates his deeds. You? Who sired two, no three, no four, National

Parks? This is an unimportant man? You stand as the visible force at the head of hundreds of pure-hearted men and women."

Each man fixed a plate and offered it to the other. They laughed and exchanged plates.

Roosevelt sat back, well pleased, "Now this is bully."

Beyond them, light glanced from eyes peering at them through tall brush.

44
A Galloping Horse
Campfire - Night 2

"I know what you want from me, John." Roosevelt paused. Muir turned his head toward the President. "Campbell's Soup."

"You have Scottish soup in your bag?" John said, surprised. "No thanks."

Roosevelt poked the fire. "You'll see. Pretty soon every house will have cans in the cupboard. Housewives will feed their families with 5 minutes of effort instead of five hours. Due to a new commercial phenomenon—Mass Brand Advertising."

Roosevelt used his hands to illustrate his points. "The Country has turned a corner, John. Big business is overtaking small industry, mom and pop stores, even farming."

Muir rose, motioned as in 'come along.'

"Businesses can make false claims." Roosevelt followed, still talking, "And the federal government is too weak to stop this."

Muir walked into the tree perimeter.

"Right now, a company could sell you tainted rat-meat and call it pork."

John interrupted, full of passion. "National Park

resources are not to be exploited or destroyed. This is by federal decree. Yet they are—voraciously."

Wa-Le-Co stepped silently behind them.

"The Smokies, shaved like a monk's head. Mesa Verde, bones of ancient people—people!—dug out and sold!"

Roosevelt interrupted in turn, "Not people who matter."

John pivoted to face Roosevelt and block his progress. "Created complicated apartments in cliffs, farmed in arid land, raised young successfully. Not matter?"

"Mesa Verde is not a National Park."

"It should be."

Wa-Le-Co could see Roosevelt's back in the moonlight.

"The Constitution," said Roosevelt, "guarantees pursuit of purpose. But if Bubba's National Meat company labels rat as pork and you rap death's door, Bubba has stolen your rights."

They each stepped into and out of small moonlit patches, black leaf shadows in relief against the cold light.

"We are both talking about stopping people who take."

"You are asking for federal control."

"No. Protection. A National Park Service—a sentinel for these holy lands."

"The US Army protects Yosemite."

"As well as they can, summers only, and they can't be everywhere. The Park is still damaged severely."

John and Roosevelt emerged from the trees to the edge of the cliff. Moonlight bathed the far steep side of the canyon.

"You have a mission, John. I appreciate that, but yours is just about uninhabited land."

"Just?" He snorted. Then shook his finger in Roosevelt's chest. "Uninhabited? Except for the millions of creatures that feed it, farm it, eat its waste, create new soil, carry its seeds, and give their own lives up to larger and larger creatures until you have something you can manfully kill."

Roosevelt was insulted. A slow burn started to show on his cheeks. Muir was strong and solid—and heedless. "And this Grand God-designed system should remain as is—unassaulted, healthy, managing itself."

"You are missing my point."

"No, you are. Native people took care of this land for 10,000 years with no more impact than a bird or a squirrel."

Wa-Le-Co stopped, rested the butt of his rifle on his foot.

Across the Valley, Yosemite Falls poured white in the moonlight.

Their tempers rose and their speech quickened. The

two men began to over-talk each other.

"Do you know what you are seeing here? The first land in the world set aside for all people—"

"Don't you see? America cast off arbitrary royal rulers—"

"Not just the elite. A complete change in land-use policy started right here."

"—Unlike other countries, we are not a monarchy."

"—But the elite are having a wee bit of trouble giving up their expectation of privilege."

Roosevelt leaned back to look at the brilliant stars. "But political bosses or Bubba can gain enough power to detour individual freedom, the same as a greedy king."

"Parks need boots on the ground."

After a small quiet pause, Roosevelt voiced, gravely, "This is my purpose, John. This is a great contest for the right of the American people to rule themselves or to be subtly hoodwinked, as powerful men get ever more adept at bypassing citizen minds to activate their baser instincts. This is my calling—to protect American citizens from soul-less monopolies. I have 6 years to get it done."

Roosevelt used his arms to demonstrate a horse, cantering, then twirled his wrist to skillfully mimic throwing a lasso. "Big business is a galloping horse. And I have to lasso it to protect the people. This is not simple, John. You want it to be."

"You are looking far ahead. So am I."

They walked, Yosemite Falls still in view.

"Think bigger, John. Monopolies are the new monarchy."

"I am thinking bigger. *You* think about this. Parks are essentially un-guarded."

"Yosemite Valley has a Guardian."

Muir's speech slowed to normal. "Ha! *A* Guardian— One man. A herd of 2000 sheep can destroy a Tuolumne meadow in a day, while the Guardian watches over the Grizzly Giant a day's walk away."

Across the Valley, a gust of wind grabbed Yosemite Falls and turned it into a dancing curtain. Both men stared, enthralled.

"People are damaging the Parks. Some for commercial purposes. Some inadvertently." Muir gestured to the sleeping canyon. "But these Parks preserve the Earth in its natural evolutionary state. This Park offers more than education and contrast, more than a place to find escape or adventure."

Muir stepped near the cliff edge. Wa-Le-Co, following, stopped. He listened.

"Parks keep the earth in balance, against the ignorant ravages of man." Muir spread his arms like a priest giving benediction. "While humans deplete their personal patches, Parks demonstrate a planet that can maintain itself."

Wa-Le-Co shook his head at himself. He sidled

closer to Muir with careful steps, closing in to an arm's length away.

"Galloping horse? It's here. It has already leapt the paddock."

"We can no longer afford passive liberty, John. As businesses consolidate and gain more power, we must prevent them from behaving badly."

"I thought you were against regulation."

"I'm against a patent medicine that poisons people. We must make the transition from passive to positive liberty.[25] Passive liberty: You do what you want. I do what I want." Roosevelt's gestures, toward John and then himself, were visible in the moonlit spaces.

"Positive liberty: If you convince a citizen to do something that will kill him, harm him, or interfere with his ability to pursue his own life-purpose, then you must be stopped.

"Passive liberty was sufficient in our early, simpler nation. But when any individual or group seeks to control others for profit or power, and they are willing to go to any length to do so, they have to be stopped if that pursuit causes harm.

"As a nation, we are turning a corner. The simplistic view of liberty won't hold in a complex society. So for now, I am intent on pointing the nation toward positive liberty—the liberty to eat food or take medicine that won't cause harm."

"We are on the same side. You are saying that the

right to profit does not supersede the right to quality of life."

"I must concentrate on a larger scale. Monopolies are the new monarchy. To expect concentrated power to behave honorably, without oversight and safeguards, gives that entity even more latitude."

"You speak of actions that endanger citizens. If the wilderness is taken, short term—and long term—health will be compromised."

Roosevelt stepped near the cliff edge. Muir joined him. Muir said, "Everybody needs beauty as well as bread, places to play in and pray in, where nature may heal and give strength to body and soul alike."[26]

Muir stepped toward Roosevelt and pointed toward Tenaya Canyon. Below, occasional lanterns illumined how very far down the bottom was. "Developers are planning to gate a section of the Valley to create a private enclave for wealthy people."

Roosevelt was not concerned. "Can't do it. It's a national park."

"Not the Valley. Like the Sequoia Grove, it's a State Park, administered by the State of California."

Wa-Le-Co again took careful steps toward Muir.

"And you think the Federal Government will do a better job?"

"The love of Nature among Californians is desperately moderate; consuming enthusiasm almost wholly unknown."[27]

Roosevelt choked on a gout of laughter. Muir slammed him on the back.

Wa-Le-Co stretched his arms forward.

"Recess California's control and make the Valley and Mariposa Grove part of Yosemite National Park."

"The federal government can't do that. California has to release it to us."

Muir threw his hands down and stomped off.

Wa-Le-Co dropped his arms. He looked over to Yosemite falls, then up to the Great Spirit.

Roosevelt walked along the cliff edge, away from Wa-Le-Co. He studied the Valley below. He peered down to El Cap, glacial polish shining in the moonlight.

Nearby, a creek tinkled. Across the silent Valley, Yosemite Falls softly roared.

"John! Come back please."

Muir's footsteps brought the man back.

"America has plenty of wild territory." Roosevelt tottered near the edge. Muir squawked, grabbed him.

"Yosemite is stalked, Sir. In 52 years, here in the Yosemite, white settlers have ruined meadows, dammed creeks, and let wooly locusts rip out native grasses."

They headed back to the campfire. Wa-Le-Co followed, listening.

"To the Indian mind all Nature is instinct with Deity. We need an organization peopled with Indian-like minds. A National Park Service."

"John, the world is now a different place and I am responsible for it. I have to say no, John. No. We have plenty of wild territory."

"Men are still crazy for gold in California. And not all the gold is the mineral buried under the earth. Yosemite *is* stalked. Make no mistake."

Back at the campfire, Roosevelt added some logs as Muir picked up the tin coffee pot. Roosevelt held forth his mug. Muir served the President and himself. "Didn't think you liked it."

Roosevelt sipped. "Am I Sequoiacal yet?"

"Not yet."

Roosevelt laughed. "You don't compromise, do you, John?"

"Give up this to get that? Appease power to get a win but lose value in the long run?"

Roosevelt's face became very serious, showing the steel behind the affability. "Is that what you think of me, John?"

The men glared at each other—a brittle face off. Roosevelt reiterated, "You are asking for federal restriction."

Muir shook his head, "No. As I said before—protection. No organization holds National Parks as a unified body. They are not, in reality, protected."

Roosevelt shook his head in a final way. "Can't do it, John. My battle is already huge. I love this wilderness. But it is not truly under threat. To establish controls in areas that are free goes against my grain."

Muir threw down his silver cup, denting it. "Unless the President needs to use regulation as a stepping stone to power."

Roosevelt's eyes narrowed. He made himself turn his inner heat down from a boil to a simmer.

Muir and Roosevelt sat quietly by the low campfire, each trying to get himself under better control.

When Roosevelt felt he'd gotten himself into a civil zone, he asked, "Would you have shot that bear to save me?"

"Yes."

Wa-Le-Co crept through woods, the campfire bright beyond black trees. He lifted his rifle, lowered it, lifted it again. Stuck the barrel through bushes.

Muir picked up his cup, wiped it on his vest, grabbed the pot, and prepared to pour.

"National Park lands are already protected by law," pointed out Roosevelt.

The conflict was immediately re-ignited.

John gestured with the pot. "National Parks are not, in reality, protected."

"You have a mission. I appreciate that."

"Sequoias store water for 100 million crops."

"That does San Francisco no good."

"Big trees are the First National Bank of water."

Roosevelt paused, then dropped the bombshell. "San Francisco needs the dam."

"What dam?"

"At Hetch Hetchy."

Muir jumped to his feet, shocked. The rifle followed him. He dropped the pot. Tea splashed up like a geyser. The fire spit and dimmed. Muir hopped around flicking off scalding drops. The rifle tried to follow. "Hetch Hetchy? It's in Yosemite National Park!"

"They've applied for an exception."

John shouted, "A dam—a huge destructive enterprise. A thousand habitats cut from the circle of life."

Wa-Le-Co aimed. Muir paced rapidly. The rifle followed him.

"10 thousand beings destroyed and the 100 thousand creatures that need them." Muir squatted and faced Roosevelt square on, in his face. Roosevelt was now between Wa-Le-Co and Muir.

"You already have over 11,000 kills. Now add Hetch Hetchy, giving yon great hunter an exceptional Kill List. Feel more manly?"

That was it!

Roosevelt socked Muir in the jaw. John fell on his bottom. Roosevelt stood. Muir scrambled up and raised his fists.

Roosevelt loomed over Muir and shouted, "I AM THE PRESIDENT!"

John dropped his fists. "I will fight you to my dying breath."

Furious, Roosevelt grabbed the shotgun. "I need to shoot something." Close by, coyotes yipped. TR stomped toward them.

Wa-Le-Co watched Roosevelt pass. Stepping toe before heel, he moved silently toward Muir.

John kicked the tin pot across the clearing. Water splashed onto the fire and dimmed it further.

Wa-Le-Co sighted on Muir.

Roosevelt sighted toward the coyote yips. His rifle clicked. No bullet. Roosevelt was greatly annoyed.

Muir kicked the logs apart, bringing sudden darkness. A log flared.

A brilliant blue Stellar Jay feather, curled on a tall boulder, glowed from that flare from the fire. As Roosevelt swiveled, it filled his sight. Roosevelt stopped, breathed.

He looked through the trees to see the last ray of setting moonlight on the side of El Cap. He made a rumbling sound, like a Scottish train sighing to a halt.

With the logs kicked apart, the clearing was black. Muir looked down, as if listening. The flare was now a small ember.

John heard Louie's voice in his mind. "Remember, John, put the man before the mission."

Muir groaned.

Roosevelt re-entered the clearing, his face open and just visible from the ember. Muir turned toward Roosevelt, really, actually, seeing him. "I was wrong—"

Roosevelt said, "You are right about—"

The last ember sputtered out. Total darkness descended.

GUNSHOT!

Boot-steps crunched twigs. Scuffling sounds. Soft patters were chased by thudding boots.

A hollow sound of wood being kicked. The snick of a flint struck.

A wee flame showed Muir bent over the logs that he'd kicked back together. He rebuilt the fire. The flame rose.

Roosevelt returned from the woods. He carried his gun. "Polecat scampered. Chased him. Lost him. Didn't see who. Too dark."

Muir grabbed the rifle. "We made a deal."

"It's not loaded."

"What were you gonna do? Knock him in the head?"

Zach thundered into the clearing, jumped from his horse, and raced toward the President. Muir, still holding the shotgun, leapt to intercept him. Zach bopped him in the jaw and grabbed the gun. Muir prepared to fight.

Roosevelt rushed forward. "No! John! This is the Treasury man. Zach! This is Muir."

Zach stepped back. "Didn't he just fire on you?"

Elias rode up.

Roosevelt said, "He wouldn't even shoot a bear with a gun."

Elias was amazed. "A bear shot at you with a gun?"

They all looked at each other. As one they curled over, hooting.

45
Sierra Forest

Wa-le-co and Man-Nik sat close to a small campfire. Their pace of speaking was characterized by a pause between each exchange, so that each message was absorbed and considered.

"I missed."

After a pause, Man-nik doubted, "You? Missed?" Man-nik looked at his nephew's fire-painted face. It was troubled.

"I hesitated."

After a pause, Man-nik asked, "Why?"

"He thinks the way we do. He's not the usual white man."

They sat quietly, watched sparks drift up.

"And, I tried three times to kill him. And failed."

After a pause, Man-nik said, "Great Spirit protected him."

Both men accepted the truth of this.

"Yes. But," Wa-Le-Co continued, "I'll never be embraced by my woman and baby when I too travel to El-o-win if I don't avenge them."

"It does not have to be him. It can be someone of his tribe."

Man-nik lip-pointed in the direction of Roosevelt.

Wa-Le-Co cleaned his rifle.

46
Is Nature Made for Man?
Night 2

Muir and Roosevelt, in their separated sleeping areas, rustled as they prepared themselves for sleep.

John called through the darkness, "Colonel. I have one question for you to ponder. It is my theme, a basis I use in my thoughts and decisions." Muir paused, then asked, "Is Nature made for Man? Or is Man made for Nature?"

Snow began to fall. Roosevelt's voice called through the night, "John!"

Muir listened.

Roosevelt continued, "If you had to choose—between getting the Valley and sequoias protected, and a National Park Service—which would you choose?"

The woods were silent. Snow fell peacefully.

47
Two Men
Glacier Point - May 17, 1903

Roosevelt and Muir at Glacier Point[28]

They awakened under a thick blanket of snow. Roosevelt laughed heartily. "This is bullier yet."

Muir and Roosevelt stood on the smooth round head of Glacier Point. *Below* Roosevelt, on the left in the distance, poured Yosemite Falls. Muir clasped his hands behind his back.

48
"Not for anything...."
Yosemite Village - Day 3

As Muir and Roosevelt rode toward the Upper Village, Villagers quickly spotted the men and spread the news. "The President is coming from the wrong end!"

Shouts relayed down the Valley. Scurrying footsteps and hoofbeats sounded as the crowd transferred itself up-Valley and thronged the bridge and the hotel.

Roosevelt and Muir looked at each other. Muir shrugged his shoulders, "Solitude done."

Roosevelt understood that it was the office more than himself personally that drew such attention. Still, he noted two things: that John was ignored completely, and that John didn't care.

Waiting outside the Sentinel Hotel, the Commissioner looked pleased as the clamor came toward them. He crowed to Governor Pardee, "After the reception, we also have fireworks planned."

Pardee, smarter than he looked, was doubtful. "This is not in accordance with the President's wishes."

The commissioner riposted, "We guess the President will do pretty much what we lay out for him to do."

Pardee commented, "You don't know him very well, do you?"

When Roosevelt saw Pardee, he rode up to him. Muir followed.

John Howard and Mr. Utilities had a good view of the entire proceedings from the corner of the second floor balcony.

Howard whistled toward the barn. Tyde, a rough-looking bounty hunter, appeared in the opening to the hay loft. He held a rifle. Howard chin-pointed toward Muir.

Roosevelt and Muir dismounted and the Commissioner and Pardee stepped up to the President. The Commissioner was expansive, "Welcome Mr. President."

"This has been the best day of my life."

The Commissioner explained, "We have a reception planned for you."

Roosevelt shook his head, "Not for anything would I miss my last campfire with John Muir."

Roosevelt stepped up on a boulder near the bridge and the people pressed in. His voice carried over the sound of the chuckling Merced River. "You are blessed to have access to this extraordinary Valley. Prophets have protected it for you. Mr. Galen Clark, Frederick Law Olmstead, Mr. Robert Underwood Johnson—"

Zach and Elias galloped up and reined their horses at the back of the crowd.

"—And Mr. John Muir."

Zach leaned over to speak to Elias. "McKinley was

shot in a crowd too."

Elias agreed, "I'm thinking about that."

Roosevelt raised a finger, "Great men aren't always seen clearly in their own neighborhood. I hope you'll open your eyes to the valiant advocate you have for this Valley in Mr. Muir."

Howard and Mr. Utilities frowned at each other. Their worst fears realized—the President admired Muir.

Zach and Elias edged their mounts around the crowd.

Roosevelt said, "I am unable to attend the reception, so please drop by and take a bit of food for yourselves and your families." Roosevelt mounted his mule and paused amid the crowd to shake hands and say low words.

Muir, astride his mule again, halted his mule next to Roosevelt's, easily above the crowd from the point of view of the hay loft.

Tyde raised his rifle.

Roosevelt shifted forward onto Sentinel Bridge. Muir shifted with him. The rifle followed Muir. Tyde's finger curled onto the trigger.

A little girl jumped up on a boulder at the side of the bridge, perfectly aligned between the rifle and Muir. Howard saw, held his breath, and then exhaled as no gunshot shattered the air. "Did you see that?"

Mr. Utilities brushed his palm sideways. "A little girl. No value in the scheme of things."

Howard froze, as he understood something about the crowd he'd thrown in with. In that moment Roosevelt spurred his mule across Sentinel Bridge. Muir followed.

The Commissioner ran after him, index finger raised. Moments, later, Tyde charged from the barn on horseback.

49
Fireworks!
1903

Roosevelt and Muir on Horseback
in Yosemite Valley[29]

Half Dome at their backs, Roosevelt and Muir galloped along the Valley road.

Zach and Elias chased them.

Tyde, boxed in by other followers on foot, horseback, and with wagons, was held back.

Muir shouted, "To Wawona!"

In the sky behind them, a fusillade of fireworks boomed.

The road curved alongside the river. Roosevelt motioned to the Treasury agents to back off. Zach and Elias pulled back, forming a barrier between the two good men and the followers.

50
A Determined Man
Terminal Moraine - 1903

On the curve just beyond the western edge of the moraine deposited by an ice age glacier, Muir took a hard right, to thread among and beyond giant boulders into thick woods. He stopped his mule, held his finger to his lips.

Roosevelt said, 'Wha—?"

Muir shook his head.

Their followers thundered on by, soon climbing the trail to Wawona.

Roosevelt started to nudge his mule. Muir lifted one hand. Roosevelt leaned back. They sat their mules, perfectly still, listening.

A raven chucked.

After a moment, another steed's gallop thundered closer, passed, then gradually faded to silence.

Roosevelt belly laughed. "You're a determined man, John."

"You have no idea, Mr. President."

Roosevelt quipped, "Actually, by now, I have a decently good idea." They listened a few more moments. Roosevelt asked, "Is there another way to get there?"

Muir answered, "I know every way to get there."

"It isn't bragging when it's true."

On the wooded horse trail, Zach and Elias leaned over their galloping mounts, panting. Zach held out his hand in a halt sign. They brought their horses to a stop.

Elias shook his head. "Don't hear 'em."

Zach turned his steed in a circle studying the ground. "No tracks."

The other men passed and thundered on up the slope.

"Not again." Zack grimaced, "If we fail—"

"—We all lose too much."

"You are finally on our side," said Zack.

"I'm not smart but I'm loyal."

They laughed together.

51

The Axe and Saw are Insanely Busy

Bridalveil Fall

Muir and Roosevelt walked up to the base of Bridalveil Fall,[30] like light pouring down the cliff. The men were silent. Roosevelt reached up to catch mist, his face awed. Muir watched—satisfied.

Muir continued to push, "I've been burned, starved, frozen, beaten, and sick to death, but nothing scares me so much as this Valley being turned into a wealthy man's private reserve."

Bridalveil
Anne Katherine

They walked the trail away from the fall, along creek-carved channels sonorous as water foamed around boulders.

Muir asked, "Do you consider a marriage license a

restriction? Or does it place something of value within a protective system?"

Roosevelt shot John a surprised look.

"The greed at nature's expense isn't here alone, you know. It's all over the world, although Europe has finally, after bitter experience, learned to value forests. But in Oregon and British Columbia, fraudulent logging companies have seized vast tracts.

"The axe and saw are insanely busy, chips are flying thick as snowflakes, and every summer thousands of acres of priceless forests, with their underbrush, soil, springs, climate, scenery, and religion, are vanishing away in clouds of smoke...."[31]

Roosevelt gave nothing away. "That is the point of having National Parks."

"Any fool can destroy trees. They cannot run away; and if they could, they would still be destroyed—chased and hunted down."[32]

The trail wound through boulders that ranged in size from a goat to 3 mammoths. Creeks, also studded with huge boulders, spread from the Fall, full of tumbling frothy water. Visual fascination in all directions.

"A news report said you called some band around here 'Dirty Indians.'"

Muir sat heavily on a boulder. "I do deserve judgment. Did you ever do something when you were young and narrow in outlook, that you later understood differently?"

Roosevelt sat on a facing boulder. He looked profoundly regretful. "They stay with you—those mistakes."

"Aye. On one of my first prowls of the canyons, Mono Indians were crossing over." Muir stood, paced to the creek.

Roosevelt followed. "I read that article. You said harsh words about the Monos, but I agree. No excuse to be filthy. Not hard to wash your face."

Muir whirled toward Roosevelt. "That's just it! I dinnae ken that black globs on faces meant grief. They were wearing the ashes of their dead. And to wash them off before a year was past was disrespectful." Muir collapsed onto another near boulder.

"In that same article you also quoted Burns."

"I did recognize, even then, that the failing was mine. 'For a' that, For a' that, It's coming yet for a' that—'"

Roosevelt completed the verse, "'That Man to Man, the world o'er, Shall brothers be for a' that.'"

Roosevelt collapsed onto another boulder. "I loved my first wife, Alice, beyond breath. She died as a result of bearing my first child, my daughter, who was named after her. And when my sister presented the babe to me to hold, I said, 'You take her. Don't ever use that name in my presence again.'"

"I wager you've figured that out by now."

"I felt I'd killed my wife. But then, so devastated, I put my blame on that blameless child instead."

Muir nodded in understanding.

Roosevelt added with deep regret, "I believe my rejection ruined her life."

The trail took them through thinning woods to a meadow carpeted with lupines, a lavender lap-robe for regal El Capitan, across the river.

"Admitting that is being a man—"

"For a' that."

Roosevelt faced Muir head on. "It's clear to me, you write what you observe, often in metaphor. But your other comment about the Mono Indians—I agree with you—Indians are lazy."

"Because their work ethic is different? The Miwok here straightened me out, and Alaska too. The Stickeen women can hardly be called loafers, for after picking berries all day, they sell them. Oh, those berries look wondrous fresh and clean. You can't mistake the kindliness of those women or their serene good nature."

"But dirty."

"The local bands smooth mud and bear grease on their faces and exposed skin to protect themselves from flies."

Roosevelt was a big enough man to shift his understanding, "Dirty on the outside."

"Clean on the inside. I daresay you know of white men with an opposite configuration." Muir gazed up at El Cap as if absorbing granite. "Speaking of which, when the white man craved gold? Right here in

California?" He bowed graciously, "Go away Mr. and Mrs. Indian." His arms lifted an invisible rifle, "Or we'll kill you." He turned to Roosevelt. "So who is it that's disrespectful toward the people who were stewards of this land for 10,000 years?"

Muir picked a lupine and threaded it through Roosevelt's buttonhole. Roosevelt stood with his chest out, tolerant. Roosevelt picked a lupine and threaded it through Muir's buttonhole. They grinned at each other.

52
"Men Must Be Judged"
Bridalveil Meadow - Night 3

Roosevelt and Muir sat alone by a crackling campfire. Roosevelt spoke, "You never mention women."

"I knew I could not be a dependable breadwinner, so I kept my distance. Then Jeanne pushed me to meet Louie."

"Did she? Curious. Few great men manage to become great without a discerning, generous woman behind them."

"Or, in my case, three—my mother, Jeanne, and my wife." Muir stood and grabbed a log from their woodpile. "And I am not great, just an ordinary man who finally found peace in following my heart and my calling."

"That is what makes a man great, John. It's the man who defends against his own heart's messages who is dangerous."

From the cliff edge, in the darkness, Wa-Le-Co overlooked the Valley, saw the campfire below.

Roosevelt and Muir sat companionably. Roosevelt poked the fire. He dropped the poker stick. "We don't agree that other races are inferior. Still, you started with your father's views and now you actually champion Indian practices."

"And you invited Booker T. Washington to the White House."

"Individuals can learn positive traits, John, just as you did. I cannot consent to take the position that the door of hope—the door of opportunity—is to be shut upon any man, purely upon the grounds of race or color."

Muir picked up the stick and poked the fire.

"Men must be judged with reference to the age in which they dwell," Roosevelt added.

John said, "I agree. I love my father. And I understand him in the context of his world."

"Despite lasting scars." Roosevelt hesitated, then risked, "I do think you missed something. I doubt it makes a difference now."

Muir sent a question toward Roosevelt.

"Mrs. Carr loved you."

"Not how I think you mean it. I'm thirteen years younger."

"Thirteen years is nothing—to someone in love. You described her passionate concern when you were blinded."

"She's married. With children."

"Regardless of convention, when someone you deeply love is in mortal danger, it's impossible to hide your distress, as her letter then revealed. And, she sent you helveticas and violets."

Muir shook his head.

"Those flowers mean undying love."

Muir looked up, appalled. "She found out about my marriage to Louie in the newspaper. Jeanne must have suffered."

Muir hung his head, in regret.

Roosevelt studied the fire, respectfully giving his friend distance. He sighed. "Men fail women. They receive female generosity believing themselves entitled, simply due to maleness."

53
Sierra Forest

Wa-Le-Co crept down a slope on foot. The voices of Muir and Roosevelt were distant but the words distinct.

"You presented me with a tough choice last night. We always have to give up something we want for something we want more."

Light reflected off the barrel of Wa-Le-Co's rifle.

54
Is Man Made for Nature?
Campfire - Night 3

Roosevelt pressed, "Do you have an answer for my question?"

"Protect the expanses of dramatic and exquisite wilderness or save the Valley that I love to my soul?"

Roosevelt nodded.

Muir answered, "We always have to sacrifice something dear for the greater good. I would have to choose for a National Park Service."

Roosevelt confided, "After my wife died, I learned that improving the lot of my fellow citizens took the sting from my own mistakes. As you said, I may have overdone it in the wild man hunter department."

Muir tried for an apologetic look that failed.

Roosevelt laughed. "You made me think. What if the world wasn't made for Man? What if Man was made for the world?"

Muir stood and paced, "The world made especially for the uses of man? Certainly not! No dogma taught by the present civilization forms so insuperable an obstacle to a right understanding of the relations which human culture sustains to wildness. Every animal, plant, and crystal controverts it in the plainest terms. Yet it is taught from century to century as something ever new and precious, and in the resulting darkness, the enormous conceit is allowed to go unchallenged."[33]

Muir sat and leaned forward, "Are birds for decorating ladies' hats? Or for singing to the trees and the flowers?"

Roosevelt gestured. "You are saying that everything is not just for our own use and comfort. I got to thinking about my dogs. My dogs are happy. I would not want it any other way."

Muir nodded, "Happiness for each one—each flower, each tree, each fish…each dog—rather than all happiness for one—man."

Muir refilled their cups from the tin on the fire, then sat. Roosevelt drank his tea in an obvious way and smacked his lips. John laughed.

"John, I see that what I have taken for lack of polish is raw character not cloaked with veneer. By not resorting to manipulation, even as threat to your mission approached, your core revealed itself. When we were at loggerheads, you did not— even then—slither."

"I sense I have passed your test."

"I didn't imagine that the man could be so divorced from his writings—but honestly, there could still have been a profit hiding behind your eloquence. I also did not see that your mission had any urgency that need involve me. But when a man is under pressure, he reveals more of himself. You know what made me truly trust you?"

"Cavorting in a glacial stream?"

"When you were most distressed, you still took care of your mule."

They headed for their bedding. Muir called, "I believe you are becoming truly sequoiacal."

Roosevelt laughed. "Now you find diplomacy."

The men walked into the darkness.

55
Sierra Forest

Wa-Le-Co turned toward the voices, now louder. The setting moon was filtered by thick lower-elevation forest and only weakly illumined small portions of the creek-carved ground.

Roosevelt called, "Before I start snoring, tell me your other favorite wild places."

Wa-Le-Co crept across the top of a granite boulder, next to the rushing creek. Rain started falling, slicking the rock.

Branches cracked as Elias, patrolling the perimeter in the dark, approached the boulder where Wa-Le-Co hunkered down. Wa-Le-Co stepped sideways and began to slide.

Muir answered, his voice fading, "Glacier Bay, the Blue Forest of Petrified Wood, Cumberland Gap, Smoky Mountains, Mammoth Cave, the Blue Ridge, Rocky Mountains, Everglades—"

56
Two Fields
May 18, 1903

Roosevelt and Muir prepared to mount their mules.

Muir asked, "I'm curious, Colonel. Will you go puma hunting with that San Francisco bigwig?"

Roosevelt rested his hand on the mule's neck. "I gave him false hope to keep him from gunning for you."

"You protected me?"

"Mayor Phelan's integrity is unquestioned. But less honorable hangers on—you are still not out of danger."

"Neither is this magnificent Valley," pushed Muir.

Roosevelt walked pointedly over to a tree. Muir's eyebrows lifted. Roosevelt gave the tree a hearty sniff. Muir guffawed.

The four men rode at a rambling walk down the trail, Elias on point, Zach on rear flank.

Muir pulled his mule up and peered into the woods. He made a distressed sound in his throat, dismounted, and headed toward a dark thicket. He returned leading an Appaloosa.

Muir talked to the horse in a low soothing voice. He pulled a pail from his kip, poured water into it, held it while the horse drank noisily.

Zach pointed to the empty scabbard and to the horse's prints. "Unshod. An Indian is nearby. Armed."

Roosevelt got it. Zach immediately looked around, into the trees, as he moved to block the President.

Roosevelt quipped, "He drew a sword in the presence of the king?"

Elias said, "That scabbard is for a firearm, not a sword."

Zach turned his mule into the woods. "I'll find him. Elias, guard the President."

Muir mounted and they let the mules amble downslope, Muir leading Wa-Le-Co's horse. As they drew closer, patriotic band music filtered toward them.

A rifle shot was followed by a pistol shot.

Roosevelt ordered, "Elias, go help Zach."

"I'm supposed to protect you."

Roosevelt eyed him in full command mode. Elias thought, mouth open, then turned his horse into the woods.

Muir brought his mule alongside the President's, purposefully riding between the President and the woods into which the Treasury men had disappeared.

Roosevelt clucked his mule forward. "Something struck me last night, John. Our names are related to each other. *Roosevelt* means field of roses. *Velt* comes from *Veldt*, and means a field. One common meaning of *muir* is from *moor*, or heath, open land."

Muir's eyes twinkled. "There is a difference."

Roosevelt cocked his head, prepared. Muir continued, "Your field is cultivated. Mine is uncultivated, left wild."

The two men hooted in laughter, yet another bond.

Patriotic music grew louder.

57
The Mountains Are Calling
Bridalveil Meadow
May 18, 1903

Crowds in their Sunday best surrounded a 4-passenger coach, Tom Gordon on reins.

Muir and Roosevelt stood beside the coach. They shook hands.

"Come see me in Washington, Friend John."

"The mountains are calling and I must go, and I will work on while I can, studying incessantly."

Roosevelt laughed and slapped Muir on the shoulder.

58
Denied!
Exclusive Men's Club
December - 1903

Howard and Hearst stood at the bar. Phelan slammed in. "The Interior Secretary denied our petition to put a dam at Hetch Hetchy!"

Howard handed Phelan a whiskey. He tossed it down.

Howard said, "We couldn't get Muir in Yosemite. So now we'll have to go after Muir's reputation."

Both men looked meaningfully at Hearst.

59
Gone
North Dome Yosemite

Man-Nik and An-Si, 15, stepped up to the rim. They looked east. And south. And west. Man-Nik shook his head. An-Si drooped. Man-Nik opened his arms. An-Si slammed into his uncle's chest and sobbed.

60
National Monuments
White House - June 8, 1906

On the desk were three brilliant blue Stellar Jay feathers, their shafts stuck into a small sequoia cone, like a small, feathery plant in a textured vase.

Roosevelt, in full Presidential togs, signed a Bill. He slammed his fist twice into his flat palm, then lifted the bill and said to the waiting pressmen, "A President can now designate protected lands as National Monuments without Congressional Approval."

61

Sound the Loud Timbrel

Let every Yosemite tree and stream rejoice![34]
Yosemite Valley - June 11, 1906

Muir faced Yosemite Falls.

He held a newspaper.

He shouted to the Falls, "Yosemite Valley Secured to Yosemite National Park. Mariposa Sequoia Grove also to become part of the National Park."

Muir, hoots of laughter, danced like a demented leprechaun.

Yosemite Falls danced too.

62
Approved!
Muir Home - 1913

Muir, 75, sat alone in front of the fire, reading a newspaper.

The paper went limp and slid to the floor.

The headline of the Hearst Newspaper screamed: "Hetch Hetchy dam approved by President Woodrow Wilson."

63

"Earth He Loved Reclaims Him"[35]

December 24, 1914

Robert Underwood Johnson wrote:

"Up through the far-flung reaches of the Yosemite, the Sequoia and all the mountain wilds of the West—

"Will ring the mournful echo of that message, for the birds and the beasts and all living things have lost a friend.

"John Muir, Apostle of the Wild, is Dead."

64
National Park Service Established

United States - August 25, 1916

Old hands hold a newspaper. "Rest in peace, my good and noble friend."

On the table beside his chair is a sequoia cone with three brilliant blue Stellar Jay feathers.

34

65
The Bones of the Ancestors
Hetch Hetchy - Some Time Past 1923

The dam is complete. The water of the reservoir begins rising.

A bone splashes to the surface.

Another bone surfaces with a pop.

Numerous bones surface. The reservoir is a floating graveyard.

Standing on the rim, looking down, is Man-nik, very old and bent. He watches the bones of his ancestors surface.

Man-Nik, crying, turns toward An-Si, who opens his arms. His uncle slams into An-Si's hard chest and sobs.

66
AMERICA

Mesa Verde

A sign is placed across a closed Gate: "It is unlawful to appropriate, excavate, injure, or destroy any historic or prehistoric ruin on Federal lands." - Antiquities Act of 1906."

Grand Canyon

A sign is pounded into the ground: "No Hunting"

An eagle soars undisturbed overhead. A child points joyfully.

Rocky Mountains

Billboards are knocked down.

"The National Park Service preserves unimpaired the natural and cultural resources and values of the National Park System for the enjoyment, education, and inspiration of this and future generations."

Beyond, is a blissful view of the peaks, an elk herd safely in the meadow below.

Smoky Mountains

Two Rangers, a man and a woman, in ranger uniforms and flat hats, ride mules up to a ridge-line and guard the land.

DEDICATED to

SUSAN ELEANOR JOHNSON

and to

LEON GLOVER

APPENDIX

I
Parks Established as a Result of Muir's or Roosevelt's Advocacy

Of course, few Parks came about from the efforts of one person alone. Many had cadres of concerned citizens making multiple efforts to create these sanctuaries.

1890 - Yosemite National Park (Muir)

1890 - Sequoia National Park (Muir)

1890 - General Grant National Park, now part of Kings Canyon (Muir)

1899 - Mt. Rainier National Park (Muir)

1906 - Petrified Forest (Muir)

1919 - Grand Canyon National Park. (Muir and Roosevelt)

1923 - Theodore Roosevelt's Birthplace

1925 - Glacier Bay National Monument (Muir)

1925 - Mt. Rushmore National Park (Roosevelt)

1926 - Mammoth Cave National Park (Muir)

1926 - Great Smoky Mountains (Muir)

1932 - Theodore Roosevelt Island National Memorial

1934 - Everglades National park (Muir)

1936 - Blue Ridge National Parkway (Muir and Roosevelt)

1940 - Cumberland Gap National Historic Park (Muir)

1947 - Theodore Roosevelt National Memorial Park

II
Postscript
December 24, 1914

Muir left the earth he loved with all his heart. Many said the loss of the Hetch Hetchy valley broke his spirit.

Hetch Hetchy proved that with enough pressure, and federal leaders willing to find loopholes, a protected land could be assaulted.

It was a warning and a lesson.

The label and designation of National Park was not enough. There had to be guardians.

It was said John lost a battle but won the war.

Just two years after his death, the Mission he'd fought so hard for became reality. The National Park Service, populated with rangers who had "Indian minds," came into being.

As a former National Park ranger, I can testify that most of us with boots on the ground are marinated in the mission of NPS, and we watch over the Parks with Muir-like intensity.

More so now than ever.

III
Remember...

*Nature's sublime wonderlands ...however well guarded...
have always been subject to attack by despoiling
gainseekers and mischief makers of every degree from
Satan to Senators, eagerly trying to make everything
immediately and selfishly commercial, with schemes
disguised....*[36]

John Muir

IV
Fact and Fiction

If you are young, it may be hard to believe there was a time that all thoughts and actions weren't broadcast to the world, but John Muir lived before Facebook and Twitter, before iDevices, videos, and recorders.

Consequently, most of the dialogue in this book is a result of studying the letters, writings, and characters of the two principals. Much of the dialogue, therefore, has been surmised, though often based on fact.

The childhood scenarios are fleshed out from John's own stories in *The Story of My Boyhood and Youth.*

John mentioned but did not often dwell on or describe the details of the beatings by his father, and he minimized, to a degree, his father's harshness.

However, in a private letter, John wrote, "In all the world I know of nothing more pathetic and deplorable than a broken-hearted child, sobbing itself to sleep after being unjustly punished by a truly pious and conscientious misguided parent."[37]

Toward the end of his life, Daniel himself spoke of his regret for his treatment of John.[38]

Muir's adult life came to be ever more documented as he began to enter the consciousness of the public and of the American leaders of the time, both political and august. Muir and Roosevelt were both prolific letter writers and, through their letters, left detailed records of their daily concerns.

While Covid terrified the world and sidelined National Park workers, I was working as a volunteer in the Yosemite Research Library.

There is a vast underground intelligence network of librarians and library workers, and the core of their mission is to connect others with knowledge. Their habit is to generously pass things around.

During Covid, libraries around the world were open to NPS library workers, paid and volunteer, for gluttonous reading and research.

Therefore, with access to the California State archives, to the Smithsonian, and to the Library of Congress, I had thousands of letters of Roosevelt and Muir at my fingertips.

I give tribute to the librarians and volunteers who digitized all those records.

Libraries create the boundaries of a civilized and educated society and recent years have underscored the importance of an educated populace.

I digress.

Fact

John Muir did walk from Wisconsin, to Canada, to Indiana, to Florida, and did catch a ride to Cuba and then to New York. He did sail from New York, go overland across Panama, and steam to San Francisco. He did walk from San Francisco to Yosemite.

John did establish six National Parks—including Yosemite, Sequoia, and General Grant, now a part of Sequoia-Kings Canyon. He did actually visit nearly all the territories he later advocated for Park status, including Mammoth Cave, what became the Blue Ridge Parkway, the Everglades, the Petrified Forest, and Glacier Bay.

John did climb all over the Yosemite.

For a good laugh, read John's suggestion for how to spend one day in Yosemite, in *The Yosemite,* Chapter 12:

If I were so time-poor as to have only one day to spend in Yosemite...

In short, climb from the Valley to Glacier Point, then onto the top of Sentinel Dome, go over to Illouette Fall, then up to Nevada Fall and to the top of Liberty Cap.

His other suggestion for a one-day excursion: go to the top of Upper Yosemite Falls, over to Eagle Peak, over to the top of El Capitan, to the top of Ribbon Fall, then down Big Oak Flat [stage-]Road.

Even one of these destinations would take more resources than the average person possesses.

If you were very fit and well equipped [and had a permit], three days [per jaunt] would allow actual enjoyment of the views.

What John would say about allotting 4 hours for a Yosemite visit, driving from one viewpoint to another for quick snapshots, then spending 45 minutes finding a place to park in order to shop or have lunch?

I'm guessing he wouldn't be tactful.

John did walk the organic perimeter of Yosemite to establish the revised Park boundary in order to protect the headwaters of all the water that entered the Valley.

His keen powers of observation regarding the formation of the Valley did contradict official opinion, especially that of Dr. Josiah Whitney, California State geologist. Whitney insulted Muir publicly when Muir insisted that the Valley was formed by glacial action.

John offered several different types of evidence, including staking the middles and edges of glaciers and checking the movement of the ice, noticing the scouring patterns, and by identifying a glacial erratic far downstream in the Merced that could only have come from one particular towering crag in the Tuolumne—and could only have been moved by the power of ice, not water. We call that Muir's rock and it is still there.

Muir's Rock
Anne Katherine

He wrote like a wilderness Shakespeare, but he was also inadvertently rude, a side-effect of his focus. Comments in letters from people who loved him, especially Mrs. Carr, indicated that they tried to guide him to be more tactful.

John was a powerfully focused man. What he loved, he loved passionately, bringing all his intelligence and energy toward learning about it.

He didn't just glance at a new flower. He sat in front of it, sometimes for days, until they had reached a communion. When he was focused on learning or, more accurately, bonding, with a new entity—whether it be an ouzel, a waterfall, or the entirety of the Yosemite—he put his entire self into it.

He had no interest in superficial time-wasters. He never pandered. And he was too straightforward and focused to curry favor.

John was interested in everything, must have had a very high IQ, and was extraordinarily competent. Had accidents and advice not narrowed his path, we'd have a very different country now.

Most of that advice came from perceptive and selfless women, especially Ann Muir, his mother; Jeanne Carr, his friend; and Louise Strentzel Muir, his wife.

Roosevelt did request John as his Yosemite guide and prominent figures of the time were enlisted to pressure John to do so.

John did initially turn them down, because he'd

planned the trip to Asia with Dr. Charles Sprague Sargent for some time, and he had a passion to personally meet every tree on the planet.

Whether his wife talked him into it, I don't know, but generally, women guided him toward his destiny.

There are two accounts of his first meeting with Roosevelt. I chose to use the one Roosevelt himself remembered as his first sight of John.

In either case, he did not show up at the reception for the President in San Francisco the night before the trip to Yosemite, though he had been summoned.

V
Fiction
Real versus Composite People

All people listed by full name were actual people in John's lifetime. An exception: his brothers, sisters, and children are listed just by first name, and were also actual people.

All people listed by first names only—except the Muir families—are fictional, at least in name.

Two secret service agents did guard Roosevelt, but I don't know their names.

They were the first full time agents. They may not have lost track of the two men, but Roosevelt did dismiss them the first day and John did pull Roosevelt away from the others to advance his agenda.

I altered the timing of the use of the small personal water-filled compass which wasn't actually available until after the camping trip.

The Burgess folding rifle and shotgun did exist—a story there too—and when Theodore Roosevelt, then president of the New York City Police Board had one pulled on him as a marketing demonstration, he enthusiastically ordered 100 guns. I have little doubt he procured some for himself.

Contrasts Between Two Great Men

Beyond their superficial differences—if contrasts in upbringing, opportunity, and social status could be considered superficial—the two men did have a fundamental disparity in their perspectives.

An apparent similarity is that both men considered and promoted conservation efforts early in their lives.

In an address to the Sierra Club on National Parks and Forest Reservations, c1894, John said, "The preservation of specimen sections of natural flora—bits of pure wildness—was a fond, favorite notion of mine long before I heard of national parks."[39]

Indeed, as an early adult, before John left his home in Wisconsin nearly for the last time in the mid 1860's, he attempted to preserve his beloved meadow and pond by buying it from his brother-in-law and funding its perpetual protection.

And that was truly before *anyone* had heard of national parks, since Yellowstone, considered the first National Park (though rangers debate this hotly), was established 1872.

Roosevelt initiated conservation of lands in North Dakota, forming the Boone and Crockett Club for that purpose.

However, peering deeper, we see the fundamental difference.

John wanted to preserve Yosemite, other grand

American lands, trees, birds, beasts, blossoms, mosses, and all supporting links in the natural chain, from his love of each entity and for their own sakes. He didn't just glance at a plant being, he bonded with it. He fell in love with trees all over the world, and with tiny wild orchids and plain birds others would overlook.

Roosevelt wanted "to promote the conservation and management of wildlife, especially big game, and its habitat, to preserve and encourage hunting...."[40]

Each man's viewpoint had value and each had positive purpose, but that divergence—love versus utility—was a powerful one.

Of course, we need presidents who can see widely, who will spread benefit across all citizens, and make no mistake, I see Theodore Roosevelt as one of our best Presidents and a truly great man.

However, he always had an eye toward utility, therefore he promoted conservation, as in the Boone and Crockett Club, to preserve land so animals would have habitat, so that those animals would thrive, so that they could be hunted.

John had important impact on Roosevelt, and one may well have been to teach Roosevelt about headwaters.

Roosevelt designated 150 National Forests. And looking closely, these all preserve headwaters. Looking more closely, these waters all sustain ranching and farm production.

Again, this is helpful: Roosevelt keeping an eye on

the link between good land stewardship, the economy, sustainable work, and feeding the nation. However, it is possible that the wealthy ranchers of the time were those most benefitted by the National Forests.

VI
Hetch Hetchy and
Other National Park Assaults

Water Rights sleight-of-hand had already been in play prior to the camping trip. Most of those in support of the dam were aboveboard. Some of those against the dam—because it would cut into their own profit—were shadier.

There were some politicians (and behind the scene puppet masters) willing to play some dirty games to make money around the Hetch Hetchy issue, and some eventually got exposed, indicted, and one, even, imprisoned.

(In completely ironic isomorphy, this water supply issue washed San Francisco city leadership clean as the bad guys were exposed and removed.)

Whether anyone went so far as to plot murder, I don't know.

It is sort of remarkable that key people in the eventual construction of the reservoir seemed to die without ever seeing the final product. But that, perhaps, is another story.

Profit-seeking men were on both sides of the Hetch Hetchy issue and some skullduggery was committed though not, so far as I know, against the President. Whether anyone was actually killed or harmed to safeguard someone's profit on either side of the issue, I don't know.

Some proponents of the dam did attempt to discredit John by saying he had cut down Yosemite trees. And that malicious rumor is still alive today. (It's amazing, how long a lie can last.)[41]

John is on record as vehemently denying ever cutting a Yosemite tree. When he ran the sawmill for Hastings, he used fallen timber, of which there is always a great deal in Yosemite.

Mayor Phelan was, by all counts, a truly honorable man dedicated to the successful future of San Francisco, concerned about a good water source, and not attending to the consequences on an area should it be harvested.

(For example, native remains were heedlessly flooded as the dam filled, with no ceremony or opportunity, so far as I know, for their ceremonial removal.)

Phelan's campaign poster[42] would

help understand this lack of empathy.

John wrote letters to both the Mayor and to the citizens of San Francisco with a clear breakdown of the additional expenses they would incur in harvesting water from such a distant source and offering alternatives that would have been far easier on the tax base. You can imagine that John was not complimentary about Phelan's intransigence.

I altered, somewhat, the timing for the interest in Hetch Hetchy, as Hetch Hetchy was among the locations considered to water San Francisco as early as 1882.

Phelan proposed damming the Tuolumne in 1890, the very same year Yosemite (including the Hetch Hetchy Valley) became a National Park.

Phelan first filed for a permit to the Department of the Interior to use Hetch Hetchy Valley for a reservoir in 1903.

Muir's letters, before he camped with Roosevelt, make no mention of a raid on Hetch Hetchy, and Muir was not shy about expressing his opinions to his friends, so I think he must not have realized the project had moved forward before meeting Roosevelt.

Roosevelt would have known this, and was on record for supporting the dam as he approached San Fransisco, so it is entirely possible that the subject came up on the camping trip, with Muir alarmed by Roosevelt and Roosevelt informed by John, because Phelan's petitions and appeals were quickly denied by Roosevelt's

Secretary of the Interior after the camping trip.

As the first President to actually visit Yosemite and one of the few to explore its interior treasures, he was also the first President to experience what was truly at stake.

In that way, John's goal for the camping trip was met.

Phelan kept after Hetch Hetchy, and his repeated efforts spurred Muir and the Sierra Club into action in 1904, with their vehement opposition beginning in 1905.

When Taft was elected, protection of Yosemite began to thin, and with Woodrow Wilson, protection was gone.

I think the Raker Act, in 1913, that created the Hetch Hetchy exception, did break John's heart and killed that great spirit, but it also served as a warning that Parks were assailable and very likely did lead to the National Park Service being established just a couple years later.

It is also true that Parks continue to be vulnerable as we've seen in recent years, with Bears Ears and Grand Staircase Escalante losing significant territory.

Obviously, I am deeply in love with Yosemite, but I think the Grand Staircase is the most important Monument in our nation, preserving as it does the entire ancient history of North America.

Exploiting and destroying those significant geological layers for fuel, especially when the Southwest has endless sun and wind for America's energy needs, is a tragic waste.

Of course the profit to be made by such exploitation is

superior to what the powerful few can glean from the infinite sun.

Trickle down? Uh-huh. You can see that in the cobbled together farms and shacks on Southwestern country roads.   Maybe enough trickles down to buy an extra 6-pack.

Oops. Soapbox and sarcasm. Or is it irony? (This is proof--I am become more Muirical.)

Still, A Reality:

When the public visits a Park that isn't spruce or efficient, it tends to blame the Park itself for crowd management or poor service or worn facilities.

However allocation of funds and policies for Visitors are not set by the Park, but by those far higher on the food chain.

The NPS budget has been decreasing for years and almost all Parks are understaffed and underfunded, while, at the same time visitation has increased.

With the understory gutted, things fall apart. Parks are not at fault for this. They don't have the resources to keep things shored up.

For example, from early in my years as a volunteer in Yosemite, the maintenance department was down 100 workers. One hundred. One guy or gal may be responsible for an area as large as two or more driving hours wide, and that area covering staff dwellings, scores of buildings and hundreds of toilets, including the rest rooms at Visitor's Centers. Just how much do you think can get done in a day?

So if you think a Visitor's Center restroom is a bit moth-eaten and shabby, look to those who fund that upkeep.

National Park foundations, the Sierra Club, the Yosemite Conservancy, and other Park-lover organizations do an amazing job filling in with money, volunteers, and programs, but those dollars can't hire more staff and, as John knew, Rangers and Volunteers, boots on the ground, are the true Guardians—the eyes, the ears, and the hearts, of any Park.

A full staff ensures a protected Park.

Oops. Soapbox.

Fiction

So far as I know, neither John nor Roosevelt was under threat during their camping trip. Whether John actually insulted Roosevelt so grievously, I don't know.

But I do believe that at the end, they were true buddies, and usually a healed conflict brings more of a bond than smooth sailing. For sure, they both respected each other highly both before and even more after.

And Roosevelt had hardly finished scratching his insect bites by the time he started keeping his word.

Fact

From Bade´[43]

Let us now recall Muir's modest excuse for postponing a world tour in order to go alone into the mountains with Theodore Roosevelt--that he "might be able to do some forest good in freely talking around the camp-fire."

It was in the glow of those camp-fires that Muir's enlightened enthusiasm and Roosevelt's courage were fused into action for the public good. The magnitude of the result was astonishing and one for which this country can never be sufficiently grateful.

When Roosevelt came to the White House in 1901, the total National Forest area amounted to 46,153,119 acres, and we have already seen what a battle it cost Muir and his friends to prevent enemies in Congress from securing the annulment of Cleveland's twenty-five million acres of forest reserves.

When he left the White House in the Spring of 1909, he [Roosevelt] had set aside more than one hundred and forty-eight million acres of additional National Forests--more than three times as much as Harrison, Cleveland, and McKinley combined!

Similarly the number of National Parks was

doubled during his administration.

John would have described himself an ordinary man, though those of us who have spent rewarding moments in National Parks, particularly those where he himself walked, would consider John Muir extraordinary.

Toward the end of his life, influential people pressured John more and more to write about his life. Here is his opinion about that:

[Now working on] *Possibly my autobiography which for ten years or more all sorts of people have been begging me to write. My life, however, has been so smooth and regular and reasonable, so free from blundering exciting adventures, the story seems hardly worth while in the midst of so much that is infinitely more important.*[44]

A smooth life?

Beaten by his father. Starving on the road. Nearly freezing in a blizzard on Mt. Shasta.

Free from exciting adventures?

Walking from Wisconsin to Florida in the aftermath of the Civil War. Traveling around the world to see the most remarkable trees. Camping with a President.

John Muir, an ordinary man, changed the world in three days (give or take 6 decades).

VII
Dedication

to

Jim Webster

Beloved Cousin:
Who lovingly affirmed each of us in his family,
Who would go out of his way, literally, to support
and give care to the many people he loved.

My Favorite Memory:
We were sitting on the deck of their house on the
Olympic peninsula, which he, his warm and
incredibly wonderful wife, Carol, and his talented
and dear son, Dan, were renovating.

Jim had been in the Coast Guard, and since I had
been Navy, we had a soft rivalry. After all, we were
both water and boat people, still. (And because of
my respect for Jim, I have respect for all Coasties.)

Jim and I shared many interests, including the
wee nestlings above his front door. Of course we
used a different door so as to not disturb the Mama
and her brood, (inconvenient when renovating a
house).

But this was the close of the day, spent enjoying

the soft summer weather, and we were chatting, never at a loss for subjects.

A nearby military base sounded *Taps*.

Without hesitation, and without words, we both immediately rose, put our hands over our hearts, and turned toward the base, where we knew the colors were being lowered.

And when the notes died away, we sat and resumed our conversation.

Jim Webster:
    A love of family.
    A love of country.
    A love of infant birds and the stars of the universe.

VIII

Grateful Acknowledgement
Yosemite National Park
Yosemite Research Library
Chief Librarian Virginia Sanchez

I spent many engrossed hours under the tutelage of Virginia Sanchez, who is passionate about books and all things library. There, over the course of ten years and counting, I was a volunteer library aide and privileged to dive deep into the world of John Muir.

With the run of the Park and access to all the Park's excellent programs, including those by the Sierra Club and Yosemite Conservancy, I was marinated in his lore and legend.

Eventually I walked and stood within all the places John camped with Roosevelt.

Yosemite's memory is long. The trees, the polished stones, and the ouzels all remember John Muir, as we always recall those who love us without qualification.

Heather Kiger

Library Guru, who linked me with valuable literary resources. (And one of my favorite people. We shared lovely moments at Yosemite, including private outrage at some Visitors who gave the grandest sights in the world short shrift.)

Library of Congress and Countless Librarians

Who spent years and tired eyes digitizing the letters of our important citizens.

Gilder Lehrman Institute of American History

My thanks for the excellent series on Roosevelt that made clear to me the difference between Passive and Positive Liberty, a distinction we are in sore need of in America today.

IX
Subtitle Team
Thanks for Contributing to the Selection of the Subtitle and Cover

Ann (Abe) B. Weston

Cassandra (Cassie) Major

Christine Gale Reynolds

Constance Wolfe

Greg Nelson

Dr. Ian Macnaughton

Judy (Jabber) Burns

Karen (Dusty) Selby

Linda Stafford

Marilyn Sherman Clay

Mark Merala

River Powers

Robert Smead

Sherry Ascher

Shirley Averett

Virginia M. Sanchez

Anonymous 1

Anonymous 2 and 3

Anonymous 4

Noble Americans, past and present, teach us how to be noble ourselves.

X
Books by
Anne Katherine

Fiction

Radical Justice

Muir

Stalking Yosemite

Soul Travel Series:

> The Yesterday Doctor
>
> Explosions
>
> The Rock Chief

Nonfiction

Boundaries: Where You End and I Begin

Where to Draw the Line

When Misery is Company

The Splintered Cross

Boundaries in an Overconnected World

Anatomy of a Food Addiction

How to Make Almost Any Diet Work

Your Appetite Switch

Lick It! Fix Her Appetite Switch

4 Changes: Fix Your Eating and Fix Your Life

Book Order Links: www.authoranne.com

XI
Ranger Anne

I've worn a variety of hats in my life—from the Brownie beanie to the Ranger's flat hat.

After 30 years as a psychotherapist, 13 years as a National Park Service volunteer in two Parks, and 3 years in the chain of command, including Commander, of a United States Power Squadron, (some of this work concurrent) I retired and became a National Park Ranger, marine certified.

I had no idea all my life experience would be required to handle the Ranger's Oath and mission:

- Protect the Park
- Promote the Visitor's Experience

At times, these were two mutually exclusive goals.

For example, if you want to pour gatorade on a

petroglyph to make an interesting photo, (your idea of a Visitor experience), I'd have to stop you to protect the Park. I'd also be protecting your experience, since harming a Park antiquity could carry a penalty of jail time and serious money, but don't worry, the maximum fine is capped at $20,000 (for a first offense).

Signaling a man speeding in a narrow channel protects the experience of other boaters, especially those in small crafts like kayaks, and also protects fragile sandstone canyon walls, but would seem to be messing with his Park experience.

A ranger makes "for the greater good" decisions constantly.

We are, also, the friendly folks in funny hats who know the names of lizards—Fred, the amazing tricks of lupines, and the answer to the very most important question—where is the bathroom?

(It helped that I was a Lifetime Girl Scout and a former camp counselor.)

My post was as Interpretive Ranger at Rainbow Bridge National Monument, which Theodore Roosevelt actually visited. In another irony, one of the grave robbers at Mesa Verde was the white man who discovered Rainbow Bridge.

Spending hours in front of that miraculous Bridge, chatting with Visitors from all sorts of backgrounds, sharing with them the geology, history, and myths about the Bridge, I came to bond with the Bridge and understand from the inside what John Muir instinctively knew: To have a powerful experience of the beauty or life of another being takes time.

Jumping out of the car, snapping a picture, and moving on, gives one only the most superficial acquaintance of majesty.

To feed your soul, stop, sit, gaze, and lose yourself in focus.

Curious at what you'll discover?

Rainbow Bridge National Monument is accessible only by water, unless you want to hike about 25 miles through the desert.

Lake Powell, the highway to the Bridge, is 200 miles long, has 99 canyons, and the water level can change 18 inches in 24 hours.

Although I had the most beautiful commute of my life, 30 minutes to two hours by boat to Bridge dock, then 45 minutes by feet to the Bridge itself, the weekend commute was a challenge.

Then the lake is packed with boats as big as a hotel, some driven by amateurs with chilled six-packs and excellent insurance.

I found that the hardest part of being a Ranger is watching people risk their lives and the lives of their children—partly out of ignorance and partly not realizing that familiarity with online videos does not render oneself experienced.

In my daily commute, I'd see scores of tragedies just

on the brink of happening.

People seemed to believe that because they were in a National Park and because they were on vacation, nothing bad could happen. I'd watch parents exercise limited judgment and know they were moments away from a frolic turning into the worst day of their lives.

But if they weren't breaking a rule, we could do nothing.

Know this: National Park rules, guidelines, and advice are not cavalier. They are always in your best interest, and a result of our broader experience.

People sometimes enjoy breaking NPS rules as a way of thumbing their noses at the government, but, believe me, your loss, if the consequences catch up with you, will be far greater than the government's.

Many of us Rangers were amazed that we had as low a body count as we did. However, it sent chills through me to hear a call over the radio for the Dive Team. That always meant recovery, not rescue.

Oops. I lapsed into being a Ranger.

Take off the flat hat. Put my author's cap back on.

An account of the challenges and some of the lives we saved will be in my TV series, *Radical Justice.* [seeking a producer.]   The book will be available soon.

Still, it was a fun job and one of my favorite parts was introducing Visitors to awe, the primary job of a Ranger. If Visitors love and respect the Park, they'll join Rangers in taking care of the Park too.

I saw first-hand that John Muir's vision of a Ranger is still alive in most of us who work the Parks, whether they be National or State Parks, whether we be paid or volunteer.

I am certain I am become more Muirical.

In 2019, Anne Katherine was honored as the Yosemite Enduring Volunteer of the Year.

Anne Katherine lives with her spouse in a National or State Park in California, Oregon, or Washington.   Find her at www.authoranne.com

Anne K. holding John
Muir's *Dented* Silver
Camping Cup

XII
Study Questions

1. John Muir and Theodore Roosevelt were unlike each other in significant ways. What were some of those differences?

2. What similarities did they share?

3. What made it possible for the two men to get past their conflicts?

4. What do you think Roosevelt admired most about John?

5. What do you admire most about John?

6. What do you admire most about Roosevelt?

7. Which of the two are you most like?

8. John Muir thought of himself as ordinary, in what ways was he extraordinary?

9. What qualities or choices did John use to make a difference?

10. In what ways are you ordinary?

11. In what ways are you extraordinary?

12. What change would you like to make in the world?

13. What choices or qualities would you need to

develop or use to make that difference?

14. Can you imagine what the world would be like had natural and wilderness and special historic places not been protected and preserved? What would it look like?

15. What is your favorite National Park?

16. What Park are you drawn to visit? (You should definitely follow that call.)

A Matter to Think About

The people of the world have had a hard time lately. Sometimes people get angry and think they need to lash out at someone or something to feel better.

One way people are lashing out is toward people in the past. When people do this, even if they are ideologically correct, they are also discharging their own negative energy, trying to feel better.

Theodore Roosevelt and John Muir are two of the people who have been targeted.

    a. What do you think about judging people for the culture they grew up in, if they knew no other way to think?

    b. If they actually are able to acquire nobler ideas than those of their family or culture—to rise above their upbringing—what does this say about them?

(You can dislike the way they think about something without rejecting their achievements, especially if those achievements bettered the lot of many others.)

Sometimes we distinguish between the way someone thinks and what they actually do—their ideas versus their behavior. Someone can have a crazy or unpopular idea, but still do a lot of good and contribute to others.

    c. If a person is kind and good to others, but believes something you disagree with, do you reject everything about them or do you separate the behavior from the beliefs?

    d. Can you think of a situation when you'd be grateful for someone's help *regardless of what they believe?*

Some people today accuse Muir based on the beliefs of some people he knew.

    e. Do you have friends or relatives who believe very differently than you do?

    f. Would you want people to judge you based on someone else's thoughts?

It's okay to disagree strongly with someone's beliefs, to hold on to your own beliefs, and still appreciate another person's basic goodness.

There is a saying, "By their fruit ye shall know them."[46]

    17. What does this mean?

XIII
Bibliographic Sources:
Works Cited

Bade, William. *the Life and Letters of John Muir*. Vols. I and II. Cambridge, MA: Houghton Mifflin, Riverside Press, 1924.

Bailey, Luther, NPS. The Strentzel/Muir home at the John Muir National Historic Site.

Meyerson, Harvey, *Nature's Army*, University Press of Kansas, 2020

Muir, John. *A thousand Mile Walk to the Gulf*. Houghton Mifflin, 1916.

Muir, John. *My First Summer in the Sierra*. Houghton Mifflin, 1911.

—. *Our National Parks*. 1901.

—. *The Story of my Boyhood and Youth*. Houghton Mifflin, 1913.

—. *The Yosemite*. Century Co., 1912.

NPS. CA, Geological Survey.

NPGallery., NPS Photo, Public Domain. National Park Service. Yosemite Park Boundary. databasin.org.

NPS, Yosemite Research Library

Roosevelt, Theodore. *Theodore Roosevelt, an autobiography*. etext prepared from 1920 edition, Scribner's, 1913.

Rose, Albert. Female Rufous Hummingbird. https://www.albertrose.com, 2021.

Thayer, James Bradley. *A Western Journey with Mr.*

Emerson. 1884.

Whitney, Josiah. *The Yosemite Guide-Book*. CA: CA Legislature, 1869. *Yosemite GuideBook*. digitized. Edited by Josiah Whitney. California Legislature, 1870.

Recommended Reading:
Son of the Wilderness by Linnie Marsh Wolfe, 1945

XIV
Endnotes

Cover Photo Credit: Anne Katherine

Maps

[1] Yosemite Boundaries. http://www.yosemite.ca.us/library/maps/#disclaimer Source: http://www.yosemite.ca.us/library/maps/yosemite_boundary_changes_1890_1964.jpg

[2] Survey Map: Credit: U.S. Geological Survey Department of the Interior/USGS U.S. Geological Survey Source: https://store.usgs.gov/product/525211

[3] Muir/Roosevelt Locations: Credit: U.S. Geological Survey Department of the Interior/USGS

[4] Hummingbird Photo Credit: Albert Rose. To order prints: https://www.albertrose.com

[5] Epigraph (J. Muir, Wild Wool, 1875).

[6] Nilya, Brian. "James D. Phelan". Densho Encyclopedia. Retrieved October 13, 2014.

[7] Study

[8] Excerpt from full letter. muir13_0290-let.tif. Courtesy of University of the Pacific Library Holt-Atherton Special Collections.

Bade', v2, p. 409. [9] Excerpt from full letter. muir13_0260-let.tif. Courtesy of University of the Pacific Library Holt-Atherton Special Collections.

[10] Referring to the age of the Sequoias—(J. Muir, The Yosemite 1912) chap 7, pp. 129,130. I added the contextual historical references.

[11] Confirmation of Beatings, (J. Muir, The Story of my Boyhood and Youth 1913), p 49, p 70, p 82

[13] Shut Your Mouth

[14] (J. Muir, The Story of my Boyhood and Youth 1913) Chap 6

[15] I found nothing to indicate that Daniel beat Ann, and perhaps John was Daniel's only scapegoat, but with Ann's love of her children, I can't imagine her not stopping Daniel without being threatened severely herself, or her other children threatened if she was seen as interfering. Later, in their lives, Daniel left to do missionary work--finally happy with his lot, and Ann was far happier then too. (Bade, Vol 2, chap 15, 1881-1891)

[16] (J. Muir, The Story of my Boyhood and Youth 1913) p 263

[17] (J. Muir, The Story of my Boyhood and Youth 1913), p 247   Daniel's attitude toward Native peoples, (J. Muir, The Story of my Boyhood and Youth 1913), pp 243

[18] Actually said by (Bade 1924), Vol 1, chap 3 1862. Such a great quote, I gave it, for just this book, to Roosevelt. It names just one of the many events that made John the man he was and that also eventually took him to Yosemite. If ever there were a demonstration of destiny, John Muir's life was thus.

[19] Carter, Quotes (j. Muir 1916) p 28, Chapter 1

[20] IBID

[21] Excerpt From: John (Muir 1916)

[22] (Bade 1924) Vol 2, chap 15 1890

[23] See first paragraphs of (Bade 1924) chap 16, in which John, 2 weeks after Yosemite is a National Park, is immediately involved in securing Kings canyon area as a part of Sequoia Nat. Park. The Roosevelt-Sequoia National Park bill is Muir's original proposal. Also described is RU Johnson's push to get a club behind Muir, hence the Sierra Club. 1892.

[24] Quote (J. Muir, Our National Parks 1901) chap 10

[25] My thanks to the Gilder Lehrman Institute of American History for the excellent series on Roosevelt that made clear to me the difference between Passive and Active Liberty, a distinction we are sore in need of in America today.

[26] (J. Muir, The Yosemite 1912) p 404

27 (Bade 1924) Vol 2, chap 15, in a letter to RUJohnson, March 4, 1890

28 Roosevelt and Muir at Glacier Point, NPS, Yosemite Research Library

29 [NPS label for photo]Roosevelt and Muir on Horseback. Photo credit: NPS, Yosemite Research Library

30 Bridalveil Fall, Photo Credit: Anne Katherine

31 Quote (J. Muir, Our National Parks 1901)chap 10

32 Quote (J. Muir, Our National Parks 1901)chap 10

33 140. (Bade 1924) Vol 1, chap 10 c1873

34 Quote (Bade 1924) To RU Johnson. Vol 2, chap XVI July 16, 1906

Appendix

35 LA Times Obituary, 1914, by Robert Underhill Johnson

36 Remember Quote (J. Muir, The Yosemite 1912) chap 16, p405

Fact and Fiction

37 (Bade 1924) Vol 1, Chap 2, Letter to a Friend, dated 2/13/1913

38 (Bade 1924) Vol 2, chapter 15

39 (Bade 1924) p 150

40 from the mission statement of the Boone and Crockett Club. https://www.boone-crockett.org, which adds: "and to maintain the highest ethical standards of fair chase and sportsmanship in North America." I could not find the date at which these additional goals were added. However, the Club also instituted a National Collection of Heads and Horns, currently housed in the National Wildlife Museum in Springfield, Missouri.

41(Bade 1924) Vol 1, Chapter 10

42 Wikipedia: James D. Phelan

43 (Bade 1924) Vol 2, Chap 18

44 (Bade 1924) Vol 2, chap 17, in a letter to Walter Hines Page, dated 1/10/1902

[45] Photo Credit: Sherry Ascher

46 Holy Bible, Matthew 7:16

9 798990 322721